Rock & Role

Read all the Cinderella Cleaners books!

MAYA GOLD

SCHOLASTIC INC.

New York   Toronto   London   Auckland
Sydney   Mexico City   New Delhi   Hong Kong

ISBN 978-0-545-12961-9

12 11 10 9 8 7 6 5 4 3 2 1   10 11 12 13 14 15/0

Printed in the U.S.A.   40
First printing, June 2010

Book design by Yaffa Jaskoll

For Jeffrey and Marc Shengold
drums and guitar

Chapter One

I know why schools stay closed all summer long. When it's sunny and hot and the sky is bright blue, the last thing on anyone's mind is geometry homework.

That goes double for hot sunny days in October, when just a few days ago it was so cold I was digging out sweaters and scarves from the back of my closet. Since my family owns a dry cleaners, where I help out after school, last winter's warm layers are spotlessly clean, wrapped in clear plastic bags. Every garment I own hangs on a paper-wrapped hanger imprinted with We ♥ Our Customers.

Today is so gorgeous that my friends and I carry our lunch bags and cafeteria trays outside for a picnic behind Weehawken Middle School. The four of us sit cross-legged on the grass with our knees almost touching, like a human four-leaf clover. I'm wearing my favorite pastel-striped tank top and skinny jeans, plus an assortment of bracelets that jangle together as I eat the last of my strawberry yogurt. I turn my face upward, enjoying the warmth.

"I love Indian summer," I sigh.

Sara Parvati digs into a take-out container of lamb vindaloo from her family's restaurant, neatly spearing a cube with her fork. "My father says 'Indian summer' means monsoon rains in Mumbai," she says.

My best friend since forever, Jess Munson, wiggles her eyebrows, holding her carrot stick like a cigar. "So should it be 'Native American summer'?" she wisecracks.

"Why don't we just call it good weather?" says Amelia Williams, practical as ever. She licks chocolate pudding off her plastic spoon with a look of pure joy. The sun shines like a halo on her straight blond hair, pulled back in a headband as usual. Jess has a wild mop of springy red curls, and Sara's hair looks like black silk. Mine is plain boring brown, like my eyes. I used to think having brown hair, brown eyes, and fair skin was wildly unfair, but I'm starting to think it's like a blank canvas: You get to create your own style. And I do.

I flop back on the grass to sunbathe, causing a chorus of groans.

"Who wants to look at your feet?" asks Amelia, and Jess says, "I'm *eating*, Diana!"

I flap my Converses back and forth, displaying their two-tone laces: my signature look, which I change all the time. Today they're hot pink and sky blue.

Sara laughs, puts down her take-out container, and lies down beside me.

"Great," says Jess. "Converses *and* sandals right in my face."

"So move your face." I shrug. My friends and I could trade good-natured insults all day, but Sara rolls onto one side, and reaches into her purse for her iPod nano.

Amelia lets out a low whistle. "Look at The Perfect One, breaking school rules!" Sara gets straight A's and once won a regional spelling bee. Amelia, who's better at soccer than schoolwork, always teases her.

"We're not *in* school," says Sara. "We're outside. Who wants to watch the new Tasha Kane video?"

That's all any of us needs to hear. We've all got different musical tastes — Jess's room is wallpapered in Jonas Brothers posters; I'm more into sound tracks for musicals — but we all love Tasha Kane. She's like Taylor Swift, Selena Gomez, and Keke Palmer rolled into one: great lyrics, great look, unbelievable dancer. And she's only sixteen.

We scramble to get ourselves into position. "Me first!" calls Amelia.

"We can all watch," says Sara, holding her nano up out of the fray.

"All four of us?" Jess bursts out laughing. "The screen is, like, the size of a gum wrapper."

"Put your head next to Diana's. Amelia, look over my shoulder."

"Um, where are our *bodies* supposed to go?" Jess asks. "Just a detail."

"Come on, we can totally do this," I say. "Scootch over."

We scootch. After trying out different positions, with a whole lot of giggling, we get our faces lined up so we can all see the screen.

"Ready?" says Sara as she presses PLAY.

The song's called "My Bad," and the video must have been shot in the Arizona desert. The colors are awesome: In the opening, Tasha's wearing a turquoise sundress and driving a purple convertible through a landscape of eye-popping red and orange rocks. Then it cuts to a concert where she's dancing and singing in front of her band, with the same colors swirling around in a light show.

The turquoise brings out Tasha's caramel skin and bright eyes. Her face is so friendly, you feel like she could be that cool girl in your class who invites you to all the best parties . . . except she's a dynamite dancer and she's, um, on*stage*.

The song has a backbeat so catchy, we all start to bounce in place. This means a lot of head-bumping, shrieks of laughter, and *ow!*s. We finally get into a groove where we're nodding and moving together, dancing on our butts. I can't remember the last time I had so much fun at lunch.

When the song ends, we all cheer. Then I notice two boys gawking at us: Ethan Thinks-He's-Cool Horowitz and Will Carson. Will is kind of a new friend and kind of a boy I might like, if he weren't so shy.

Will's tall, with dark hair that always seems to be falling in front of his eyes. Ethan's shorter and stockier, with blue eyes and a dent in his chin that makes him think he's supercute (and apparently some girls agree). Ethan is cracking up at the sight of us. Will's only smiling, but knowing he watched me rock out with my friends makes me blush like a dork.

"What were you geeks watching?" Ethan asks.

"Tasha Kane's new video," says Sara. "It's *sick*!"

Ethan groans. "Girl pop!"

Will raises his eyebrows. Is he going to make fun of us, too? Boys don't tend to get Tasha Kane; it's a girl thing. But Will just says, "Yeah? Did you like it?" He's looking at me.

We all answer at once, drowning out Ethan's jeers. Amelia says, "Great!" at the same time as I say, "Way cool." Jess gives a little shrug and says, "Fine," in a tone that implies she's heard better, which is a little annoying, considering she was so into the song that she banged my head twice. Sometimes Jess takes her Jonas fandom so far she has trouble admitting she likes other singers, too. There is such a thing as being too loyal.

"I *love* Tasha Kane," Sara says dreamily. "If I could be anyone else in the world for a day, I'd be her."

"I heard she's shooting a video somewhere near here," says Amelia.

Really? My heart races. That would be unbelievable!

Sara's dark eyes, which are pretty big anyway, get even bigger. "No *way!*"

"Way. One of Z's bunhead friends even tried out for it." Amelia's big sister, Zoe, is as into dance as Amelia is into sports. She takes ballet, modern, and hip-hop at three different dance schools.

"Why didn't you tell me?" says Sara, indignant.

"I did. I just did," Amelia says calmly.

"Are they making the video in New York City?" I ask eagerly. Like any actress, I'm always eager to hear backstage gossip. Zoe's friend is so lucky. Imagine getting to try out for a rock video!

Amelia shakes her head. "Nope, they're shooting it right here in Jersey. But no one knows where. It's all very top secret."

"Well, duh," says Jess. "They have to hide Tasha from stalkers like Sara."

Sara's too excited to notice the sarcasm. "We have to find out," she says, bouncing in place like a kid who's had too much birthday cake. "*Have* to."

I notice that Will looks uncomfortable. What is it about girls being fans that makes guys so self-conscious? It's not as if we expect them to start shrieking and giggling with us, hello. Anyway, Will is a rock fan himself. He plays bass guitar in a band, and in the two months he's gone to our school, I don't think I've ever seen him wear a T-shirt without a band logo or photo of some classic rocker. Today's shirt says WILCO.

"Don't believe every rumor you hear," Ethan says. "Why would Tasha Sugarcane come to Weehawken, New Jersey?"

"Easy," says Jess, tossing back her red hair. "She must have a crush on *you*."

"What, you think she's got taste?" Ethan grins.

"More than you've got," Jess shoots back as the bell rings for class.

"Oops, you set off the fire alarm. Must be your hair," Ethan says.

"Well, it's not your lame burn."

They could do this for hours. In fact, sometimes they do. But as we start scooping up wrappers and trays, Ethan's girlfriend, Kayleigh Carell, sticks her head out the door, calling his name as if it's two separate words: "*Eee!* Than!" Brushing her long blond hair back from her face, she shoots him a look that clearly says, *What are you doing with those losers?* Never mind that Jess and I have known Ethan since preschool, and Will is his best friend, and we're all in the drama club: Kayleigh wants him to herself.

Ethan lumps over to join her, muttering under his breath, "Yeah, yeah."

Will doesn't follow. I don't think he has any more use for Kayleigh than Jess and I do, another reason I might kind of like him.

My next class is English, the only class Will and I have together. Sara's in it, too, but Amelia and Jess have Spanish.

I wonder if Will's going to walk me upstairs. If so, will he *talk*? Will is really quiet, especially one-on-one. When Jess and I saw him play bass with his brother's band, I couldn't believe the relaxed and confident rocker onstage was the same Will Carson who slouches around Weehawken Middle School, walking too close to the lockers. I'd wondered if he would act differently after we'd seen him perform, but as soon as he went back to school, he got tongue-tied again. I can relate. When I'm in a play, I'm a whole different person. I actually know what to say if you give me a script.

Will and I look at each other. "It's a shame to go back inside when it's so nice out," I say in a voice that sounds way too chirpy. I can't believe I just said "It's a shame." I sound like a guidance counselor. Will nods, watching a maple leaf fall to the ground.

"At least it's for English, right?" Will nods again and we head for the door to the stairs. If I want conversation, clearly I'm going to have to make it myself.

We're reading *Romeo and Juliet* for class, which I'm really enjoying, since our English teacher's a frustrated actor and likes to read scenes from Shakespeare out loud.

"Did you finish reading Act Two?" I ask Will, just to fill up the silence again.

Will says, "Uh-huh." Oh my god, it's a *monologue*! I smile to myself as we head up the stairs.

As soon as school's over, I take the bus to my father's dry cleaners, where I'm an after-school helper. It's not an official *job*, since I'm still underage, but it is what my stepmother calls "a commitment." As in, something I have to do every day, whether I want to or not. But it's turned out to be much more fun than I expected, because I love fashion and clothes . . . and because you never know what's going to happen when you walk through the door of Cinderella Cleaners.

It's a short walk from the bus stop, and I take my time, trying to memorize the feeling of sun on my skin, in case the weather remembers it's supposed to be fall and drops back down to frosty tonight.

Cinderella Cleaners isn't in much of a neighborhood: mostly fast-food drive-throughs and gas stations, with a few self-storage units and warehouses on the side streets. Right next to the cleaners is a vintage chrome diner called Sam's, which looks just like it did when my grandfather took me there for Shirley Temples. Papa used to tell all the waitresses I was the princess the neon crown on the roof of Cinderella Cleaners was made for. "Extra cherries for this one," he'd say, patting the top of my head.

I cut through the parking lot between Sam's and the cleaners. It still gives me a thrill to go in through the employee entrance, like a real insider. I stash my backpack in my locker, pin my name tag onto my smock, and go into the workroom. The machine noise and chemical smells don't startle me like they used to. I've got it *down*.

The first thing I do every day is report to the only employee I *don't* like — wouldn't you know it, my supervisor. Miss MacInerny won't let me call her by the name on her tag, which is just as well, since I couldn't look at her tight-lipped frown and say "Joy" with a straight face. My friends Catalina James and Elise Andrews take turns working with MacInerny at the customer counter. I'm protected from this, since I'm too young to run the cash register, but I can't help wondering what will happen next week when Elise goes on leave for basketball season. Will Cat be stuck working with Joyless all day, every day? Will I have to learn extra jobs in the back to fill in? I know Dad isn't hiring a part-time replacement, since money is tight. In fact, ever since I overheard him talking with his accountant, I've been keeping my fingers crossed that my buddy Nelson Martinez, the head tailor, won't get laid off.

Elise flashes me a smile as MacInerny greets me with her usual sucking-on-lemons face and a brusque "Good afternoon." Somehow, with just two words, she makes me feel like I'm late when I'm not, or that I've already messed up something I haven't started yet. I had a math teacher like that last year. You were guilty until proven innocent.

There's a cart full of clothes that need to go back to the workroom, so I assume that'll be my first job. But before I can roll it out, MacInerny hands me a man's jacket and says, "Bring this to Tailoring."

I smile. Any workday that starts with a visit to Nelson is fine with me. Then I notice the cuffs are rolled up inside out, with safety pins jabbed through the fabric — the customer must have marked it himself. "Nelson's not going to like this," I say. "He'll want to measure it on the customer."

"Nelson's not here," MacInerny says curtly. The breath goes out of my lungs as if someone just punched me. Nelson couldn't have been fired that fast. Could he? Maybe she just means Nelson's not here *today*. Maybe he's out sick or something.

"Where is he?" I ask, but MacInerny has already turned toward the next customer waiting in line, flashing her fake-friendly smile. I look at Elise, who shakes her head, clueless. That makes sense. She comes to work straight from high school, arriving just minutes before me, so how would she know?

Clutching the jacket, I carry it into the tailoring section. Nelson is nowhere in sight, but both white-haired seam-stresses look up from their sewing machines. "Hello, gorgeous," Sadie says, and then turns her head toward Loretta. "Is she a vision or what?"

"She's a vision," Loretta rasps, nodding.

In my smock? Not quite what *I'd* call a vision, but okay.

"Where's Nelson?" I ask.

They look at each other. "Haven't you heard?" Sadie says.

"Heard what? Where is he?" I'm starting to panic.

"The word is he's taking some 'personal time.'" Sadie

raises both hands from her sewing machine, crooking her index and middle fingers into quote marks.

"What does that mean? Is he coming back?" I'm so upset I can barely control my voice. How could Dad *do* this? Nelson is not just the head of the tailoring section, he's its heart and soul. Loretta and Sadie have great sewing skills — they've both worked here for decades — but Nelson's the one with the designer's eye. He's the go-to guy for fixing things, even when they seem impossible. And he's my friend. I can't stand the thought of working at Cinderella Cleaners without him.

"You know what we know." Sadie shrugs. "Personal time, and I quote."

"Such a talented boy," says Loretta. She holds out her hand for the jacket, frowning. "What kind of klutz pinned these cuffs?"

I ask everyone in the workroom if they've heard anything more about Nelson. The rumors are flying. He quit, he got fired, someone made him an offer he couldn't refuse.

When Cat gets in she's as upset as I am. Nelson's her best friend at work. He designed both our dresses when we got to sneak into opening night of the Broadway show *Angel*. He and Cat love to gossip and crack jokes in Spanish. His family is Cuban, and Cat's mother is from Guatemala, so they're both totally fluent.

"I can't believe he'd take off without saying *hasta luego*," Cat says. "That's not like Nelson at all." She looks as if she's going to burst into tears.

That does it. I put down the orders I'm sorting and march to my father's office. I need to get to the bottom of this.

Dad's sitting at his big desk, holding the phone to his ear. He's probably on a customer service call. He winks at me, gesturing that I should sit, but I don't.

"Yes, of course," he says into the phone. "I understand. . . . Right. I'll send somebody out right away." He rolls his eyes at me, letting me know that he's talking with someone who's being difficult. "Of course. Not a prob-lem. . . . Well, that's what we're here for." He hangs up and sighs. Then his face brightens. "How are *you*, honey?"

"Where's Nelson?" I ask, getting right to the point.

"He's taking some personal time," says Dad automatically.

"What does that *mean*? Did you fire him?"

Dad looks insulted. "Of course not. He told me he needed some time to pursue other projects, and I let him have it, even though he gave no notice at all."

That's a surprise. This was Nelson's idea?

I look closely at Dad. He wouldn't lie to me. Not about something like this. "So that means he'll be coming back, right?" I ask hopefully.

Dad sighs. "I suppose that depends on the other proj-ects." He isn't meeting my eye, and I can't help remembering the conversation I overheard between him and his accoun-tant, Morris. I heard Morris advise Dad to let someone go, and suggest "that tailor Martinez."

"Did Nelson say what he's doing?" I press.

"Diana, I've said all I can. It's enough." So he does know more, but he's not going to tell me. I can read my dad like a book, and he knows it. He's studying me as if he's considering something. Maybe if I look angelic enough, he'll tell me everything.

Dad leans back in his chair. "Can I entrust you with something?"

Oh, good. Here it is. I nod eagerly. "Sure!"

"I just got off the phone with a client. You know Lydia Felter?"

I nod. Everyone knows Mrs. Felter — she's here twice a week in her silk blouses and power suits, always making some special demand or complaining about something somebody did wrong. But what has that got to do with Nelson? Is he doing some special project for *her*?

Dad goes on. "She dropped something off for her daughter this morning, same-day service, and can't pick it up by the end of the workday. I need someone to walk it down to her building. It's only a few blocks away — you know RiverVista Estates?"

Of course I do. Has Dad forgotten how much Mom hated those condo developments, with their tall towers and penthouses blocking the view for the rest of us? When I was little, she dragged me to committee meetings and sat at the ShopRite with petitions to Stop RiverVista. I hated going to those boring meetings then, but if I could have even an hour of that time with my mother again, I'd never complain about anything.

Dad misunderstands my hesitation. "You don't have to go up to their penthouse, just drop it off with the doorman downstairs. Or I can ask Cat or Elise."

"No, it's fine," I say quickly. The truth is, I'd love to go for a walk in the still-warm weather and clear my head. And even if I hate those condos, their view of the Manhattan skyline is stunning. I never get tired of seeing that sight. And dreaming of Broadway.

Dad smiles. "That's my girl." He opens the door of his office and leads me out to the customer counter. "Diana is making a special delivery," he announces to Joyless. "She'll be back in a half hour or so."

I slip out of my smock as Dad steps on the pedal that sends the conveyor belt of bagged clothes swishing around the ceiling. I used to call it the Dress Parade when I was little. I wonder what pantsuit or stiff evening dress Mrs. Felter needs ASAP. Dad stops the belt and takes down a clear plastic bag. My jaw drops.

Inside is the cutest vest I've ever seen. It's dark blue with a deep scoop neck, tiny lapels, and a pieced satin back, with a row of adorable miniature buttons. It's totally not Mrs. Felter's taste — I'd wear it myself, maybe to a concert or a party. Where did she *find* it? And why did she buy something so trendy and hip? Then I remember Dad telling me she'd dropped it off for her daughter.

Lucky daughter.

Dad prints the receipt and shows me the address. "Nikki Felter," he says, handing over the vest. "That's Lydia's daughter. Got your phone?" I pat my pocket, and he gives me a hug, saying, "Have fun." I take special pleasure in going outside through the customers-only door, right under Joyless's nose.

The breeze catches the plastic bag like a sail, and I drape it over my shoulder, hooking my thumb through the top of the hanger. I haven't gone ten steps away from the cleaners when I run smack into the last person I'd ever expect to see on this corner:

Will Carson!

Chapter Two

Will is coming from Sam's Diner, holding a cardboard tray full of cups. We stare at each other in shock. Then I blurt out a line that's so obvious I'd groan if I had to say it in a play: "What are you *doing* here?"

Will's answer isn't much better. "Um, getting drinks?" He holds the tray up for proof. Funny, I guessed that part.

"Thirsty much?" I say.

Will looks confused or uncomfortable, I can't tell which. Did he not get the joke? I point. Two milk shakes, a Coke, and a coffee. Oh, never mind.

"Who's all that for?" I ask.

"Oh. Just some people. My dad." He looks nervously

over my shoulder. "So this is where you . . . I thought you worked closer to school."

"No, I take the bus." Boy, *that* was interesting. Shy must be catching.

Will nods, shuffling his feet as the wind blows his hair across his forehead. He reaches up, brushing it off, and it blows right back down. "So, see you later, I guess." He starts to walk past me, and looks almost worried when I head the same way.

I lift up the hanger, explaining, "Delivery. Where is your dad?"

"He's . . . um, over there." He makes a vague gesture toward the river.

"Me, too!" I blush. "I mean, that's where I'm *going*."

Will nods, but says nothing. We wait for the streetlight, then cross and walk most of a block without saying a word. I'm racking my brain for some way to make conversation. "Isn't your dad a musician?"

"Yeah." Silence. We keep on walking.

"What instrument?"

"He was a drummer."

Was? "What is he doing now?"

Will stops walking suddenly, turning to face me. "Can you keep a secret?" he asks. I'm so surprised by his intense gaze that I just nod. "It's a really big secret," he adds. "Like, *huge*."

"I swear," I say, wondering what it could be. I'm excited. "I won't tell anyone."

Will takes a deep breath. "He's a sound engineer."

That doesn't seem like much of a secret. I look at him, waiting for more. Will sighs. "On Tasha Kane's video."

My eyeballs bulge out of my head. I shriek, "WHAT?"

"You promised," Will says quickly. "You can't tell *anyone*."

"Your father is working with *Tasha Kane*?" I'm about to fall over, right on the sidewalk. Huge doesn't cover it. This is beyond huge; it's epic. I look at the tray full of drinks in Will's hands, and blurt, "Are those for *her*?"

He grins. "No way. She's got a P.A. to take care of her." I'm proud to recognize the inside slang for Production

Assistant. "These are for the crew in the sound booth. Dad's posse."

Somehow we've started walking again. My heart's pounding high up in my throat and my mind's full of so many questions, I don't know where to begin. I can't believe someone I know — and let's face it, who I sort of like — is hanging around in the sound booth for Tasha Kane's video! No wonder Will's expression looked weird when Amelia and Sara were talking about Tasha during lunch today. My friends would totally freak if they knew!

I'm totally freaking myself, but I don't want to show it, especially when Will seems so chill with all this. He's actually gotten less mumbly and shy — he seems as relaxed as he was with a bass in his hands onstage. Maybe just being around music makes him open up.

"So where are they shooting?" I ask, and Will darts me a look. "I won't tell, I swear. I already promised." It's got to be close by, since Will is on foot.

"The soundstage is inside a warehouse. They're keeping

it all under wraps because Tasha gets *mobbed* by fans. You can't imagine."

Actually, I can. I was backstage at a Broadway opening and saw all the fans leaning over the rail to get autographs from Adam Kessler, the star. Tasha's about six billion times more famous, though. Magazine-cover-and-Grammy-Award famous.

"How did your dad get to work for her?" I ask.

"He's friends with her manager. That's why we moved here from Santa Fe." Will has stopped walking. He's standing outside the old Standard Carpet warehouse, which looks . . . like an old carpet warehouse. If they're trying to keep a low profile, they're doing a wonderful job. I notice a few glossy cars parked on the street, and some new-looking bolts on the side entrance. Could it be?

I point over Will's shoulder, raising my eyebrows. He nods. "But you really —"

"I know," I say quickly. "Your secret is safe with me."

He looks at the dry-cleaner bag I'm holding over my shoulder. "How far do you have to take that?"

I swivel and point at the glass and chrome tower that looms from the skyline a few blocks away. "The HideousVista."

"So would you have time to . . . I mean, if you wanted . . ." Why is he mumbling *now*? I'm holding my breath. Could he possibly mean what I'm hoping?

Will looks down at his feet, takes a deep breath, and raises his eyes to look right into mine. "Do you want to come in with me?"

Oh. My. God.

"YES!" I burst out, about five times as loud as I meant to. Will looks as if he's having second thoughts. I better curb my enthusiasm a little, but I have to ask. "Will I get to *meet* her?"

"No way," Will says quickly. "We'll be inside the sound booth. It's one-way glass, so Dad lets me and my brother hang out and watch if we want. But he's really serious about not getting in the star's way, ever, ever."

I nod. I understand about artists and privacy. I'm an aspiring actress, after all, not some clueless fan girl. "Got it," I tell him. "I'll leave her completely alone."

"Promise?"

Will looks a little unsure, so I say it again. "I totally promise."

"Okay, then come on," says Will, and we start toward the door. I'm so excited I feel like I'm going to trip over my feet. That would be classy.

Another breeze catches the cleaner bag and I realize I'm going to feel like an idiot taking it into the soundstage. But what can I do? I can't very well hang it out here on the chain-link fence. Someone might steal Nikki Felter's supercool rock 'n' roll vest, and then I'd be in serious trouble. Unless . . .

"What is it?" Will asks, and I realize my steps have slowed.

"I don't want to bring this inside."

"Oh," says Will. "I don't think anyone cares."

I care. If I'm going to meet Tasha Kane — which *might* happen, even if we're in the sound booth — I don't want to be clutching a dry-cleaner bag. And I'd like to show *some* sense of style. I glance down at the boring striped tank top and skinny jeans I pulled from my dresser this morning.

And if I put on Nikki's vest, no one can steal it. Right?

"Just a minute," I say to Will, and before he can ask what I'm doing, I've hung the bag up on the fence, reached inside it, and shimmied the vest off its hanger. I slip it on over my tank top. It fits as if it were made for me.

"Cool," says Will, and leads me to the door. As we get closer, I notice a state-of-the-art security camera and intercom system you wouldn't find on most buildings designed to store shag rugs. I hold Will's tray of drinks while he punches in a code and gives both our names to the intercom. The door buzzes open. Standing right inside are two massive security guards. It's just the way I pictured a movie set entrance would be. I get actual goose bumps.

"You, I got," says the first huge guard, nodding at Will. "You're Tyler Carson's kid. Who's your company?"

"A friend from school," says Will. "She knows the rules."

I nod, feeling nervous. "I won't bother Tasha, and I won't tell anyone."

"Word," says the guard. "'Cause we've got you on camera." He jabs his thumb at the security monitor, where our whole interaction is playing on staticky black-and-white.

"I swear," I say.

"Sign in," says the guard, and I do. The second guard passes a metal detector wand over us. He's not at all scary — I don't think Will and I look like much of a threat — but I'm extra glad I didn't bring in a dry-cleaning bag on a wire hanger.

"Okay, you're cool," says the guard. "Keep it quiet, they're taping."

They're *taping*? Wow! This is amazing! I still can't believe I'm here.

Will leads me down a hall with a lot of doors. Where do they lead? Who's behind them? This feels so *back-stage*. Finally we get to a door with a red light above it. Will and I pause. I can hear one of Tasha's recordings being played — at least that's what I think I'm hearing, till someone says, "Cut!" and the music stops. The red light goes off.

31

I look at Will, wide-eyed. That was *live*!

"Quick," he says. "They're between takes." He swings open the door to the sound booth, and we slip inside.

The booth is much bigger than I would have guessed, filled with racks of recording and mixing equipment. The whole front is glass, and the scene I can see through the window looks like something out of a DVD special feature. There are lights set up all around the band, and the lead guitarist is mopping sweat from his forehead with a bandanna. The drummer is chugging a bottle of water. There are crew guys in baseball caps, camera technicians rolling their rigs back into place for the next take.

And right in the center of it all is Tasha Kane, standing patiently still as a makeup girl brushes blush onto her face.

She can't be more than ten yards away. I stare at her, mesmerized by every detail. She's wearing a peacock blue top over leggings and ankle boots, with a studded black belt and a really cool necklace that looks like a giant charm bracelet. Her hair is pulled back from her forehead with a triple-strand headband, and tumbles around her pretty face in a pile of black curls. She's shorter in person than I would have guessed, and her skin is the color of butterscotch toffee. Even standing still, she's magnetic. I can't take my eyes off her.

Will slides the cup of coffee in front of a man who must be his father — they have the same arching eyebrows. Mr. Carson is wearing a headset, and his face is lit by rows of controls. He mouths a quick thanks while listening to somebody over the headset. "Got it," he says, rubbing the bridge of his nose. "Yeah, I'm on it." He moves a few levers on a control panel that looks like it might fly a jumbo jet. Memo to self: Ask Will exactly what his dad *does* as a sound engineer. It sure looks important.

Will passes a milk shake to a technician with shoulder-length dreads, and the Coke to a woman in a black tank top, with a dragon tattooed on one shoulder. He comes back to join me, taking a sip from the second milk shake. "Want some? It's vanilla." He holds out the cup.

Only a boy could think about food at a moment like this. I shake my head, still studying Tasha. How can she stand still, doing nothing at all, and still give off this vibe of being a star? It's incredible.

Will smiles. I can tell he's enjoying my view of his world. It's hard to imagine that this could be somebody's version of visiting Dad at the office. It makes watching the Dress Parade seem pretty puny.

The drummer runs a stick over the snare drum, pumping one foot up and down in a trickle of rhythm. All three cameras are back in their places. An English-accented voice that must be the director's comes over an intercom. "Right, then, let's do another. You good to go?" he asks. Tasha nods, and the makeup girl scurries off to the sidelines. A young woman holding a clapper slate — just like the souvenir one I have in my room, with the black-and-white striped bar on top — takes her place. I hear a familiar set of commands that I've only heard in movies before: "Roll tape. . . . Rolling. . . . Action!"

And suddenly I'm at a Tasha Kane concert! The bass

and drums slap down a dance beat, the keyboard player joins in, and Tasha starts strutting and singing, her unmistakable voice sounding just like it does on the radio. The song has a chorus so catchy that I want to sing along with it the first time I'm hearing the words.

"Have you heard?" Tasha sings. *"Have you heard, heard the word?"*

One of the cameras is swooping around her as she sings and dances, and a man with a microphone on a long pole follows every move she makes. How can she concentrate with all that equipment so close to her? She really is a pro. And her dance moves are awesome.

"Cut!" says the voice on the intercom. Everything shuts down at once. Tasha looks frustrated. The drummer groans. Inside the booth, the guy with the dreadlocks slumps back in his chair and says, "What are we on, take sixteen?"

"Sorry, people," the director says through the intercom. "Camera glitch. How about a ten-minute break?"

"Make it fifteen," Tasha says.

"For you, darling, twenty," the voice replies.

"All *right*," says Will's father, stretching his arms. He turns in his swivel chair, smiling at me. "Welcome to the exciting world of recording. Five seconds and sixteen takes."

"This is Diana," says Will. "From school. She works at the cleaners right next to the diner."

"Oh, sure," says Will's father. "I dropped off some shirts there last week."

For the first time since we came inside, I remember I'm supposed to be running an errand. A quick one. "Oh, yeah . . . I better get going," I tell Will. "My dad'll get worried if I'm gone too long."

"It's a dad thing," says Mr. Carson, winking. "Nice meeting you."

"Thank you *so* much," I say. "This was amazing."

Will puts down his milk shake and opens the door of the sound booth. As we step into the hall, I'm shocked to see a familiar peacock blue top coming right toward me. I gulp.

It's Tasha!

I can't believe she's standing just four feet away. She looks as beautiful close up as she does from far away, but she's shorter than me! I gasp like a goldfish that just got pulled out of its bowl.

Tasha smiles vaguely at Will like she's seen him before, but isn't quite sure of his name. She gives me a quick glance in passing, then turns and looks back with an intent expression.

"Cool vest!" she says. "Where did you get that?"

Blushing bright red, I stammer, "Um . . . it was a gift."

Well, sort of. And then I can't help myself. I know I promised to leave her alone, but she talked to me first, and it bubbles right out of my mouth. "I totally love you!"

Oh, help, could I sound any stupider?

"Your music," I babble, embarrassed. "I totally love your songs."

"Thanks," Tasha says in an offhand way — not rude, but like you might say "Bless you" if someone sneezed. Her eyes are still fixed on Nikki Felter's vest. She turns to the young Asian woman beside her, who must be her assistant. "See this, Rachel? This is the look I want Ingrid to do. Can I bring you to Wardrobe?"

Wait . . . is she talking to . . . me? That's impossible. I must look totally dumbstruck, because Tasha says, "Sorry, I don't know your name."

"I-it's Diana," I manage to stutter.

"Diana." Tasha Kane smiles. "Follow me."

I hesitate maybe a split second. Yes, I am already late to drop off the vest, and yes, Dad's going to worry, but she's *Tasha Kane*! I can't believe that I'm *talking* to her, let alone following her to the wardrobe department. She's chatting about some scene in the video where that vest would be *perfect*. Her assistant, Rachel, walks beside her, nodding at every word. Maybe it's her job to nod.

Will follows a few steps behind, looking like *he* can't believe this is happening, either.

Rachel opens a door and Tasha strides into a room full of costume racks. She gestures to me and says, "*This* is exactly the look I was talking about for the scene with the schoolgirls."

The man leaning over the cutting table looks up, and I get the shock of my life. It's Nelson!

"What are you *doing* here?" I sputter for the second time this afternoon.

"I could ask you the same thing." Nelson grins. "Are you spying on me?"

If Tasha's surprised that this stranger she dragged down the hall knows the costume assistant, she doesn't let on. "Where's Ingrid?" she asks impatiently. "I want her to see this vest. And Diana's shoelaces."

My heart skips a beat. Tasha Kane thinks my two-tones are cool!

"Ingrid's out," Nelson says. "Why don't you model for me, Miss Diana?" He picks up a digital camera, ushering me toward the three-way mirror with a big smile on his face. Except for the megastar standing six feet away, it feels just like old times.

Nelson places me right in the center. "Straight pose," he says, clicking. I try my best to pose naturally while my heartbeat goes out of control. At least the vest feels good on me. Nelson takes several more shots. "Okay, try another one. Work the look. Pose it."

He takes more photos, his grin so infectious that I can't help grinning right back.

Tasha turns toward Rachel. "She's got great energy. Do you act?"

Again, it takes me a beat to realize that she means me. But Will answers for me. "Yes, she does."

Tasha nods. "Bring her in for the schoolgirls," she tells her assistant. "Don't they have callbacks for extras tomorrow?"

"Yes, but the main thing they're still looking for is the Indian girl."

"Indian girl?" I blurt out. "My friend Sara Parvati is Indian!"

"Bring them both in," Tasha says to her assistant. And off she goes, leaving Rachel and Nelson both staring at me in the mirror. What just happened?

Nelson's grin gets even wider. "Hey, Cinderella. I think you just scored an audition."

My mouth drops open, just like a cartoon. Is this real? It can't be!

The door swings back open. It's Tasha, and she's pointing straight at me.

"Oh, and Diana? Be sure you wear that vest!"

Chapter Three

Wear that vest. Those three words clang in my head like a fire alarm as I stand beside Nelson, Rachel, and Will in the wardrobe room. How can I wear this vest when I'm already late to deliver it to the person who actually owns it?

I'm in big trouble whatever I do. If I don't bring the vest to Nikki Felter right now, what will I say to Dad? How can I tell him it's taken me forty-five minutes to *not* do the errand he trusted me with?

But if I do go and make my delivery, (A) I'll get back even later, and (B) what am I going to wear to the audition tomorrow?

B is the killer. I'm still having trouble grasping that I've even *met* Tasha Kane, never mind been asked to try out for her video and told what to wear. I'm so busy turning it over frantically in my mind that I barely notice that Rachel has whipped out her cell and is talking to someone.

"No, they're not SAG or AFTRA, they're just local teens. . . . Well, what are your numbers on background?" I have no clue what this means, but there's no mistaking the next part. "Look, just bring them in as a favor to Tasha, okay?"

She looks at me. "I need your names for the casting director."

The *casting director*! My heart starts to pound. "Um . . . Diana Donato and Sara Parvati. Sara with no *H*, her full name's Sahira."

Rachel repeats our names into the phone. "Parvati. Right, for the Bollywood girl . . . Got it. Bless you." She hangs up and looks at us.

"Okay, they're squeezing you in at the tail end of call-backs tomorrow, at six-thirty."

I can't believe my ears. "Here?"

Rachel looks at me like I'm an idiot. "*Nobody* knows about this place, and nobody can. It's tip-top security. You and Sahira cannot tell a living soul about this project till after we've wrapped, and *especially* not where we're shooting. Get permission from your parents, signed, and that's *it*. Are we clear?"

I nod. "Will already told me. I swear I'll keep quiet."

"Six-thirty sharp at the Holiday Inn, conference suite B. Tell the hotel desk that you're being seen for the lip gloss commercial. No mention of Tasha Kane, or you're right off the list."

Wow, I think, nodding even more vigorously. This is like being a spy. If it's this complicated for girls trying out to be extras, what is it like to be *Tasha*? She's only three years older than me. I can't imagine not being able to go anywhere without being followed by fans. I mean, what if she just wants a hamburger? And how does she *date*?

But I don't have time to think about Tasha Kane's problems right now. I've got my own bumper crop of them.

Rachel leaves, and the second the door swings shut, Nelson holds out his fist to me and we bump knuckles. Nelson says, "Score!" Then he turns his head toward Will. "And you are?"

"Oh, this is Will," I say quickly. "His dad's in the sound booth. And Nelson works at the cleaners."

Should that be in past tense? I certainly hope not. "You *are* coming back, aren't you?" I ask him.

Nelson gives a mysterious smile. "That depends," he says. "I could get used to this, but the designer?" His eyebrows raise into the disapproving expression I've seen at the cleaners when someone drops off something hideous.

"Ingrid?" I ask.

"Yes, Ingrid" — Nelson's face changes seamlessly as the door opens — "will definitely want to look at that vest." He glances up, feigning surprise as a woman with bristling platinum-blond hair and high cheekbones sweeps in. "Here she is now."

"Vest?" Ingrid frowns.

"Tasha loves this one. *Loves* it," says Nelson. I get the sense there's a history to this discussion, and sure enough,

Ingrid darts a look at a dressmaker's dummy wearing a much less appealing vest. The table beside it is littered with sketches.

Ingrid circles me, eyeing the cut. "May we borrow?"

Oh, no! I send Nelson a desperate eye signal, and he steps behind me to take off the vest, running his thumb along the inside of the collar where there's a telltale Cinderella Cleaners tag. In the three-way mirror, I see just the barest hint of a smile on his lips. Nelson knows me too well.

"I'll cut a pattern that I can *copy* and get this back ASAP," he says, weighing his words as he looks at Will. "*Someone* will drop it off where it belongs. Right, Will?"

Will nods.

"Thank you so much," I say gratefully. "I've got to run." Nelson is the greatest. He *has* to come back to the cleaners!

As I charge down the sidewalk, my mind floods with questions. Can Will manage to get Nikki's vest to her building before Mrs. Felter gets home? Will Nelson really be able to sew me a duplicate vest by tomorrow? Will Dad even let me audition?

There's no way on earth not to tell him — the six-thirty callbacks are right after work, exactly when Dad would be driving me home. And if by some miracle I *do* get cast, I'll need his permission — and that won't be easy to get if he knows I snuck into the tryouts behind his back. Sara will have the same problem: her parents are strict, and she works Friday nights at their restaurant, Masala.

They *have* to let us try out! It's just off-the-planet incredible that we've been offered this chance, and even if they're *parents*, they have to understand that.

I'm way out of breath by the time I rush into Dad's front office, gasping out, "Sorry I'm late."

He looks up from his desk and says, "Who was that boy?"

"What?" I say. How did he *know*? He must have spotted me walking away from Sam's Diner with Will. "Oh. Just a friend from school."

I feel myself blushing. It's *true*, so why do I feel like I'm lying?

Dad takes in my breathlessness, flushed face, and shining eyes. It's totally clear what he's thinking, and I'm so embarrassed, I get even redder.

"I called you three times," he says. "What good is your phone if you don't turn it on? I've told you and told you."

I shut the door tight and perch on the edge of the chair by his desk, leaning forward.

"You'll never believe what just happened," I tell Dad. And I pour out the whole story (minus the part about wearing the vest, of course): how I ran into Will in the parking lot, and where he was going, and that I met Tasha Kane, and that I have an audition, tomorrow!

"So can I go? Please? I'll do anything! Please, Daddy!" I haven't called him that since I was little. It just slips out.

Dad leans back in his desk chair, studying my face. He looks proud and fond and a little bit worried — that "how did you get so grown-up?" mix that parents pull sometimes. I can't tell which part will win out.

Dad lets out a sigh. "Well, it's all right with me." OMG! He's going to let me go! I can't believe my luck!

"But . . ." My heart freezes. Here it comes. "I'll have to ask Fay."

"You can't!" I blurt without thinking. Dad's whole face changes. He looks disappointed and angry. Everything about me and my stepmother is such a minefield. One tiny false step, and it all explodes.

I have to fix this, and fast. "I don't mean because she'll say no." (Though she will. Always does.) "I'm not allowed to tell *anyone*. The whole project's top secret. I promised I wouldn't —"

"Diana —" he starts, but I'm too desperate to stop talking.

"I *had* to ask you, and I know you'll keep my secret, because . . ." The answer comes into my head at the exact moment I need it. "Because you kept Nelson's."

Dad looks at me. "You saw him there?"

I nod. "So you must have heard all about the security issues. You know I'm not making this up." I meet his eyes, pleading. "It's not that I don't trust Fay. But you've seen the twins' room." My nine-year-old stepsisters, Ashley and Brynna, have Tasha Kane posters all over their bedroom — she's like their new Hannah Montana. "Can you imagine if they found out? They'd tell every nine-year-old girl in New Jersey!"

Dad takes his time answering. I hold my breath as he sighs. "I don't like secrets, but I see your point. We will need to keep this from Ashley and Brynna."

I launch myself into his lap, hugging and thanking him. His desk chair swivels, nearly toppling me off, but I don't care. "Dad, you rule!"

"But I am telling Fay."

"What?" I pull back and stare at him. "You just said —"

"That I won't tell the girls. But Fay is my wife, and your stepmother. I won't keep this a secret from her."

"You know she won't let me! That's like saying no, except you're making her be the bad cop."

"I'm sorry you feel that way," Dad says stiffly. He sounds really hurt, and I realize that sounded harsh.

"It's just that Fay always says no to me. It's like she thinks it's good for my character, like I'll be a spoiled brat if I get what I want."

Dad sighs. "We have different parenting styles."

That's one way to put it. For the ten millionth time, I think, *Why did you have to get married again?* And why did it have to be *her*? There are so many things I could say, but I can't think of one that won't hurt Dad's feelings, so I just keep quiet. That turns out to be the right choice.

"All right," he says. "Here's what I'll do. I can see this is very important to you, and you've been a good sport about giving up drama club and coming to work at the cleaners. I am telling Fay, because it's the right thing to do. But I'm not going to ask her permission. I've given you mine, and I will stand by that." He holds up his hand with the knuckles half curled. "What's that handshakey thing you kids do?"

I straighten his fingers, touch his palm with mine. "High five." Then I curl them and give him a knuckle bump. "Pound."

"Got it," he says with a smile. My dad is the best!

· · ·

I bring my cell phone into the one truly private place in Cinderella Cleaners — the fur storage vault, which is quiet and cool, with a door that shuts tight.

Sara picks up on the first ring. "Amelia?"

I can hear music in the background — the same Tasha Kane song she played us at school, "My Bad." This makes me smile. "Nope, it's Diana. Are you by yourself?"

"Yeah, I'm doing my homework."

Right after school, when it's gorgeous out? That is so Sara Parvati. "Are you sitting down?"

"I'm lying on my bed with my laptop. Why?"

So you won't fall over, I think. I'm enjoying this. "Promise me — swear up and down, cross your heart and whatever — that you'll keep this secret. Like, *nobody* else can know. Promise?"

"Of course," Sara says, and I tell her I met Tasha Kane. Her scream is so loud that I almost go deaf in one ear. "No way," she keeps saying. "No freaking *way*! I'm listening to Tasha *right now*!"

"I can hear her."

"You *met* her? Where? What was she wearing — no, what was she *like*? Tell me everything. How did this happen? Where? When? Did you actually *talk* to her?"

"Better than that," I say. I tell her about Will and his dad, and seeing Tasha from the sound booth. I save the best for last: our audition.

"No way! Are you pranking me? You better not be, I'll kill you!"

"I'm totally not pranking. But it's tomorrow, and we need our parents' permission."

"Oh, they're going to give it," says Sara. "No matter what. I'll do chores for the rest of my life. Scrub the restaurant floor with a toothbrush. I'm *going*."

She will, too. When Sara sets her mind on something, you might as well try to stop a tornado. I'll have to be like that with Fay, who I'm sure is going to pull out every trick in the book to override Dad. I'm not missing out on this chance, and that's that.

I feel better already. When I leave the fur vault, the radio's playing "My Bad." The maintenance man, Chris, bobs his head as he empties a lint trap.

"I *love* this song," he says, and I grin. That makes two of us.

I float through the rest of the afternoon on a cushion of joy. I don't care how many tasks MacInerny throws at me, or how fast I have to work to make up for lost time. I haven't been so excited since I went to see *Angel* and met Adam Kessler. Two stars in two months! And both of them happened because of this job. If these are the perks, I'll work at Cinderella Cleaners forever.

Even the having-a-secret part's fun. I look over at Cat, who is running a Brooks Brothers suit through the bagging machine as she sings along with "My Bad," and think, *I'm trying out for a Tasha Kane video — tomorrow!* I can't stop smiling.

"Okay, so who is he?" asks Cat.

"Who?" I say, startled.

"Whoever is making your eyes look like fireworks." She hangs the suit up on a clothes rack and folds her arms. "Don't try to fool me. I know you, remember?"

Did Cat see me leave with Will, too? She couldn't have — there are no windows in the workroom. Besides, my glow is all about Tasha Kane, but I can't set Cat straight about *that*.

Our drama club advisor, Ms. Wyant, taught us how actors tap into their own real emotions to channel something their character feels. It's called "sense memory." If you use something real in your acting, it's going to feel real to your audience, too. That little flutter I feel around Will could come in very handy right now.

"Okay, fine. I was doing an errand for Dad and ran into this guy I might like," I tell Cat, and her eyes open wide.

"*Might* like? That looks like a four-alarm crush."

Am I blushing again? I wish I had Sara's complexion. It's so embarrassing having a face that's a billboard for every emotion. But useful for acting.

And that's all I'm doing, right? Acting the part of a girl who got caught with a secret crush. Looks like I pulled it off well, because Cat's grin gets even wider.

"Okay, I won't ask any questions, like who is he, how do you know him, where you ran into him, is he cute, do you have any pictures?"

I can't help cracking up. "But you're not going to ask any questions?" I love Cat.

"Two words," she says. "*How* cute?"

Tonight's dinner is one of Dad's favorites: chicken marsala with mashed potatoes. The twins don't want icky brown mushroom sauce on their chicken, so they're eating chicken nuggets instead. There's also a big bowl of string beans, the only green vegetable Ashley will touch. Fine with me; I love string beans.

Truth is, I could eat a dog biscuit tonight and be happy. I'm so excited that I'm afraid Fay, who's got very good radar, will catch on that I'm hiding something and ask what it is. Dad and I have agreed that he'll tell her about my audition tonight, when the twins go to bed. I try pulling up a sense memory of my last French test to flatten my mood, but it doesn't help. Then I think of something that actually does burst my bubble a little: Jess.

Jess and I have been best friends since grade school. Mom used to call us two peas in a pod, which was funny, because we look nothing alike. Jess calls every night at the same time, and we fill each other in on whatever part of our day we haven't already spent with each other. She's been keeping me posted on drama club gossip all fall, and I fill her in on the people she's met at the cleaners. But lately our every-night calls have been way more about Jess than me. This is because Jess likes a boy we both met at the Foreman Academy dance, and he likes her, too. Which is huge. So our conversations have been full of "Jason said this, Jason texted me that, Jason posted a new profile picture on Facebook," and my dialogue has been mostly "Uh-huh . . . Really? . . . Great."

But tonight I've got huge news myself, and I can't breathe a word to my bestie. That pulls the corners of my mouth back down to a normal position, at least long enough to do dishes and homework. When I head upstairs to my room, past the twins' open door, and look in on their bunk-bedded Tasha Kane shrine, I start grinning again.

"What are you staring at?" Ashley says, folding her arms like an nine-year-old ninja. Brynna looks up from the bottom bunk, where she's reading a sparkly lavender book about unicorns.

"Nothing," I say. "Have you heard the new Tasha Kane song?"

"'My Bad'?" Ashley says. "Of *course.*"

"It's awesome," says Brynna.

It is. It is totally awesome. I go up the stairs two at a time, reminding myself to go into their room and borrow something for Tasha to autograph. After I get the role, that is.

In my room, with the door closed, I allow myself to really get into the fantasy. I turn on my laptop, which still has a screensaver of Adam Kessler, and put on some YouTube clips of Tasha's videos. I watch every one of them twice, then replay my favorites as a sound track for picking my outfit.

Ms. Wyant told us that you're supposed to dress the same way for a callback as you did the first time you were seen, because if they're calling you back, it means they liked your look for the part. Of course, I don't know what "the part" is, but Tasha said something about schoolgirls, and she liked my two-tone shoelaces. So I guess I'm supposed to just dress as myself. Plus a fabulous vest. Thank you, Nelson!

I fluff out my hair and put eyeliner under my eyes, smudging it a little like Captain Jack Sparrow. I put on my favorite acid-wash skinny jeans and a tank top I think will work well with the cut of the vest. I pick out a belt to wear low on my hips — it looks more rock 'n' roll that way. Then I start trying on bangles and necklaces from my Accessory Wall. I'm making a pile on my bed when the phone rings. It's Jess.

"Hello?" I already feel guilty. I have to remind myself that she can't see what I'm wearing. But I could be dressed in a clown suit for all Jess would notice.

"Guess what," she demands, her voice bursting with news.

"What?" For a moment, I hope she'll say, "*That's* what," an old gotcha game we used to pull on each other when we were little. But she's too excited.

"Jason asked me to go to a movie with him!"

"You're kidding me! When?"

"Next Friday!" Her voice is unnaturally high, like she's turning into a hamster.

"Is it, like, a *date*?" I ask.

"I don't know. I've gone to the movies with friends. Even guy friends," Jess says. "What exactly would make it a date?"

That's a really good question. "Is it just the two of you?"

"Remember that girl you pretended to be at the boarding school?"

"Annika Reed?" Of course I remember; her name and uniform got me past the Foreman Academy gates. She turned out to be really cool.

"Annika, right. She'll be there. And Jason invited you, too. Can you come?"

"Of course." This is really big news. In spite of their constant texting and Facebooking, Jess and "the fourth Jonas," as we've nicknamed Jason, have been together in person just one time, the night they first met at the Foreman Academy dance. "Are you nervous?"

"Good nervous. Excited. Like, ready to burst."

She definitely sounds it. Her voice is still an octave too high, and I feel a bubble of jealousy. I try to imagine Will asking me out to a movie, even with friends going, too, and can't picture it. Even if he liked me that way, which he totally doesn't, he'd be way too shy to pick up the phone. Jason must really like Jess, I think, feeling disloyal for envying her. It's not like I don't have my own great news. Which I can't share with Jess.

"That is so cool! So what are we seeing?"

There's an odd little pause. "I forgot to ask." Jess sounds as if she can't believe it. Neither can I. She's a movie fanatic, the hardest to please when a bunch of us go to the multiplex for bargain Sundays. She must really like Jason, too.

"Diana? If it's, like, an actual *date*, not just friends going out to the movies, does that make Jason my . . . *boyfriend*? Are we *going out*?"

I don't know the answer to this either. None of these words has a definite yes-or-no meaning. Some eighth graders tell everyone they're "going out" with guys that they've never gone anywhere with, or call someone their boyfriend the first time he says hello. We need some words for all the shades of vague that come between "Single" and "In a Relationship" on Facebook status. Those "kind ofs" and "sort ofs" can make you insane, even if you're not already preoccupied with a killer audition tomorrow.

"What do you think?" says Jess. But before I can come up with something that passes for wisdom, Fay knocks on my door.

"I need to speak with you," she says. My heart drops like a stone down a well.

"Later," I tell Jess, and hang up the phone. I sit on the edge of my bed, take a deep breath, and tell Fay, "Come in."

She does. She's still dressed in the outfit she wore to her realty office today — a cream-colored pantsuit and tangerine blouse with a matching silk scarf — and the contrast between that and my rock 'n' roll outfit is kind of funny. I hope she won't freak at the smudgy black eyeliner. I was just fooling around.

My stepmother runs her eyes over my bedroom — the ceiling collage of old *Playbills*, the scarves and jewelry dangling from nails on my Accessory Wall — and I sense her Realtor's eye deducting the value of being Not Neat. She takes in the piles of discarded clothes on my bed and the floor, and her mouth gets tighter. "I'll pick it all up," I say quickly. "Before bed."

Fay gets right to the point. "Your father told me about this audition."

I nod, holding my breath. *Did he tell you I'm going, whatever you say? Because I am.*

"Frankly, it sounds like a waste of your time. Why would Tasha Kane pick someone like you when there are so many professional actors your age?"

Thanks for the big vote of confidence, Fay.

"Well, I guess stars are flighty," Fay goes on before I can answer. "Don't get your hopes up. You're just going to be disappointed."

"I just want a chance to try out," I tell her, though of

course I'd also love to get cast. Didn't she ever want something she knew was a long shot? For the first time, I wonder what Fay was like when she was my age. I don't really know much about her, except that her family was poor and she had to work hard from the time she was young. I don't even know what color her hair was before she started frosting and spraying it.

Fay looks at me evenly. "I don't see the point, but you're not missing school or your job, and your father's already said yes. So I'm just going to ask you one favor."

Oh, no. Here it comes. If she tries to stand in my way, I will throw such a fit. Dad *promised* me I had permission. It's not up to Fay. I don't care what she says. I set my jaw into a straight line and stare at her, waiting.

"If you do get to see Tasha Kane, could you get her to sign some T-shirts for Ashley and Brynna? Those would make the perfect Christmas presents for the girls."

Of all the things I didn't think she would say, that might be the top of the list. "Of course!" I say, grinning from ear to ear. "Thank you, Fay!"

"Thank you for what?" she says. "I didn't do anything."

Exactly. Thank you for not interfering. I'm so happy I don't even mind when Fay turns at the door and adds, "Clean up this room. It's a pigsty."

Chapter Four

I get dressed for school in my cool rocker outfit, minus the eyeliner, bangles, and belt, which I stash in my backpack. I'll put those on later, along with the vest Nelson is making for me.

Jess is not at our corner, which means she's running late, as usual. When I get to her house, Mrs. Munson is bouncing around the small kitchen in flowered scrubs, throwing cold cuts on bread and carrots in ziplock bags. I watch as Jess and Dash finish inhaling their breakfasts, drop dishes into the sink, and shove homework and lunch bags into their backpacks. It's like being inside a pinball machine.

Dash jumps on his bike, and Jess and I practically charge up the hill, with barely enough breath to talk about movie plans with 4-J (aka the Fourth Jonas). But luckily we make it to school while the buses are still letting out.

Sara spots us from across the parking lot and runs over. Either she's never heard of playing it cool or she really can't act. She swoops down on me with her eyes shining and grabs my arm, jumping up and down like a hyperactive kangaroo. "I'm soooooo pumped!" she gushes.

Jess looks at her like she's gone off the deep end. Which maybe she has. "About what?"

Sara realizes too late that she shouldn't have acted like that. She looks totally guilty, then makes it worse by going too casual and saying, "Oh . . . nothing," in that see-through way no one ever does when it really *is* nothing.

Great, I think. She's kept this a secret for all of five seconds. I look Sara right in the eye while explaining to Jess, "Dad's taking me to Masala tonight after work." Which is actually true. I just left out a few details. Like that we're not going for dinner but picking up Sara and driving her *to the audition for Tasha Kane's video*!

Sara looks awed, like she's just figured out I'm an actress. She nods.

"Isn't that cool?" I ask Jess, who looks puzzled by Sara making such a big deal over dinner at her family's restaurant.

"Cool," she says. "Order the curry with meatballs."

I breathe a big sigh of relief. Solved *that* problem!

My first class is gym, and as soon as I see Amelia in the locker room, calmly pulling on an Emily the Strange T-shirt and sweat shorts, I start to relax. If Sara had broken her word and told someone last night, it definitely would be Amelia, her BFF. But Amelia has nothing more on her mind than destroying the opposite team at crab soccer.

I hate crab soccer. If people were meant to travel around on our butts, we'd be built upside down. And kicking the ball from a sitting position? Forget about it! Amelia is actually *good* at crab soccer, and scores every goal for our team. Any game with a ball and two teams makes her happy. I guess it's her version of being onstage.

I manage to make it through gym, but as soon as I have to sit down in a science class, my mind starts to race. How could anyone think about photosynthesis at a time like this?

I wonder what music video auditions are like. I'm sure there won't be any dialogue to perform, since Tasha said we would be extras. What will the schoolgirl extras actually *do*, and why did the casting director need a "Bollywood girl"? Will we have to do dance combinations, like in *A Chorus Line*? Will there be *cameras*?

I'm dying to ask Ms. Wyant what to expect, and slow down as I walk past the classroom where she teaches sixth-grade English. But I can't say anything. I promised Will, I remind myself as I speed off to my locker.

I don't see Will all morning, but I spot him outside his locker before lunch. His dark bangs flop into his eyes as he fiddles with his combination. Today's T-shirt is red, with a logo on the back for a band I don't know, Hallway Passage. He looks up and sees me.

"Hey," he mumbles.

"Hey." Now I'm getting as tongue-tied as he is. What gives?

Will shuffles in place. "Everything cool for . . . you know?"

I nod eagerly. "I am so stoked," I whisper.

"Cool," says Will, pulling open his locker. "Oh. Here." He reaches inside for a black plastic bag that's jammed in at an angle.

I don't have a clue what it is. I open the plastic bag up and my stomach drops into my sneakers. Inside it is Nikki Felter's vest, rolled up in its dry-cleaner bag!

"Why do you have that?" I gasp.

Will looks puzzled. "You said to deliver it."

"To the *customer*, not to me! It had to get to her doorman by six o'clock yesterday. That's why I was walking it over."

Will's face falls. "Oh. I'm really sorry, I —"

"It isn't your fault, it's mine," I say quickly. "I totally wasn't clear. I should have told you the details, but the costume designer . . . Ingrid . . . was in the room with us. And the customer's address was right on the tag — I thought Nelson would know what I meant . . ." I trail off, angry at myself for the miscommunication. Never assume someone will get what you mean when it's really important.

Will looks really worried. "Will you get in trouble?"

Of *course*. Dad will be furious, but I don't want Will to feel any worse. "It'll be fine," I say, trying my best to sound breezy, but he sees right through me. People keep doing that. Acting in real life is so much harder than acting on stage.

"I messed up," Will says, sounding really unhappy.

"It's nothing. After what you did for me? I never thought I'd get to . . ." I notice Will looking nervously over his shoulder, as if he's afraid of who might overhear us. "Well, you know."

Will nods. He *does* know, I think gratefully. Who would have guessed quiet Will was a person who got to hang out around rock stars? Still waters run cool. I'm dying to ask him more about his father's job and what other celebs he's met. I wonder if he's ever gone to the Grammy Awards. "Are you going to lunch?" I ask.

Will shakes his head. "Band practice."

"Oh. Okay." I'm actually disappointed. This is getting ridiculous. I mean, it's not as if he's Adam Kessler or Zac Efron or someone like that. He's just Will. My friend. Who might have some cool stories to tell. That's all.

"Later," he says, ambling off toward the band room. I look down at the plastic-bagged vest in my hand and think, *Help*.

My heart's heavy with dread as I ride the bus to the cleaners. I can't figure out if it's better to bring the vest straight to Nikki's doorman, so I can tell Dad it's been delivered, or bring it to the cleaners so he can see for himself it's not damaged or missing. I decide the second way is safer. For one thing, it's already almost three o'clock, and I don't want to be late for work. And if I deliver Nikki's vest to her later, I can stop by the soundstage on my way back from the condo and pick up the duplicate vest from Nelson.

Assuming there *is* a duplicate vest. If Will and Nelson misunderstood what I meant, maybe I misunderstood

Nelson, too. It all happened so fast. And why would Nelson take time to sew me a copy? It's not like he owes me a favor; he's more than made up for the time I covered for him when he borrowed a customer's tailored silk shirt from the cleaners. And he must have plenty to do in Tasha's costume shop.

What if this was just wishful thinking, and I have to audition in just my own clothes? Tasha looked more at the vest than at me. Would she even know who I was without it?

I put that thought out of my mind. One disaster at a time. I've got plenty to go around.

Sure enough, as I walk from the bus to the cleaners, the first thing I see is my father waiting for me. He's standing behind the front window with his arms folded, and the stenciled crown design on the glass makes him look like an angry king. He signals that I should come through the front entrance and straight to his office.

This is bad. Really bad.

"What did you do with that vest?" he says without greeting me first.

"I'm so sorry," I say, handing over the black plastic bag. "Will brought this to me at school. I guess I . . . kind of left it behind."

"You left it behind," he says, staring at me. "At this video shoot?"

I nod, squirming. "Where?" Dad demands. "On some table somewhere?"

I make the split-second decision to tell him the truth. I'm in too much trouble already. "In the costume shop."

"When you saw Nelson?"

I wince. The last thing I want to do is get Nelson in trouble, too. "It was Nelson who found it. He told Will to return the vest ASAP, but Will thought he meant to return it to *me*, not the cleaners."

It's kind of the truth, though I left out the part where Nelson asked if he could keep it to copy the pattern. It's better if it looks like my fault, like I just spaced out and forgot all about it.

Dad reaches into the bag and takes out the vest. It's been folded over the hanger, still inside its dry-cleaner bag.

"I'll deliver it now if you want," I offer.

Dad holds up the bag. The crumpled-up vest hangs down in a sad, wrinkled clump. "Diana, does this look like something we can deliver as is? We'll have to steam-press and rebag the garment. Then I will be taking it straight to the customer, with apologies and a gift certificate."

"I'll pay for it," I say quickly.

He looks at me. "Yes, I think that's a good plan. I was thinking of two hundred dollars."

Two hundred dollars! It'll take me forever to earn that much! Well, it'll be worth it if Dad lets me go to auditions. I don't dare to ask, but I have to know. "Dad? Can I still go tonight?"

"What do you think?" He's got that I'm-disappointed-you-even-asked look on his face, but I can't let this go. It means much too much to me.

"Dad, do you know how amazing it is that I even got asked to try out? And it's not fair to Sara. You can punish me later, however you want, but Sara can't get to auditions without me. Both of her parents are working tonight, and she's never tried out for anything, not even a school play. She's counting on me."

Dad gives me a long, even look. He's not one to yell, but when he gets angry, his voice drops down low, like a rumble of thunder way off in the distance. "You don't understand what a mess this is, Diana. Lydia Felter's been calling all day. She's threatening never to use Cinderella Cleaners again. She's been a major client for years."

"I know," I say, hanging my head.

"No, I don't think you do know. I don't mean her personal clothes, though we dry-clean those, too. She's our corporate contact at Garden State Catering."

I sit bolt upright. "You mean . . . ?"

Dad nods. "All those linen tablecloths, napkins, the waitstaff's tuxedos. They cater events every week for every hotel conference and wedding reception in north Jersey. We depend on that income."

I feel about two inches tall. How could I be so stupid? I know more than I should about Dad's money woes. If the cleaners lost Garden State Catering, Nelson might never come back. Or worse. What if we had to shut down? What if everyone who works here lost their jobs, just because I thought I had to look cool to meet Tasha Kane?

"I'm so, so, so sorry," I say in a small voice.

"I believe you," Dad says. "But that won't solve the problem."

I nod. There's a lump in my throat that makes it hard to swallow. "So . . . I guess I better call Sara and say I can't come."

Dad looks at me for a long moment. "I didn't say that," he says.

My eyes open wide. Is he changing his mind?

"It wasn't entirely your fault," he says. "I shouldn't have trusted you with an errand that mattered this much. You're thirteen years old. And you're right about Sara. She didn't do anything wrong, and she's relying on us."

Us. He said *us*.

"So . . . does that mean you're still willing to drive me and Sara?" I ask, barely daring to hope.

"I don't condone what you did. But you told me the truth, and you offered to pay Mrs. Felter. I appreciate that very much."

Dad sits on the edge of his desk. The anger is gone from his face. He looks tired and sad. I hope he's not going to talk about Mom; I might burst into tears. I can keep it together most of the time, but when I get overemotional, Mom always comes right to my mind. Especially when I'm around Dad, or my grandparents. I have a sudden sharp stab of missing Papa and Nonni. I wish they still lived in New Jersey instead of in Florida, that they still worked at the cleaners.

Dad rubs the bridge of his nose. I notice his hair's getting thin at the temples. "This transition has been hard on everyone," he says quietly. "I know you miss having your afternoons free with your friends, and I wish I could give you that back. I wish you didn't have to grow up quite so fast. But I do need your help at the cleaners."

"I love working here," I say quickly.

Dad looks surprised. "Really?"

I nod. "Really truly. Don't ever feel bad about that. I want to help out. I'm just sorry I caused such a problem."

"Well, then, let's try to fix it," he says, suddenly brisk.

He hands over the vest. "Take this back to get pressed right away, and I'll call Mrs. Felter. Again."

I turn back at the door. "Thank you so much, Dad. I love you." He's already picked up the phone, and gives me an impatient wave, but I know my words have made him happy.

On my way back to the dressing room, I give the vest to Mr. Chen at the pressing machine, telling him it's a priority rush job. He nods and gets right to work.

I stash my school backpack inside my locker and glance at the time as I pull on my smock. Three hours from now, we'll be driving to Sara's to pick her up for the audition! My heart starts to race at the thought, so it feels like my whole body is humming a tune.

But when can I pick up the duplicate vest that I'm now praying Nelson has made? Clearly, Dad's not going to take any more chances on me as a delivery person, and I can't blame him. So I'll have to wait till my afternoon break to sneak down to the soundstage.

But that doesn't work, either. Today is Elise's last day before she starts training for basketball season, and Cat's insisting that the three of us take our break together. She's been training Lara Dodichek, a young woman who works in the back, so they can trade off at the customer counter while Elise is on leave.

"Lara can cover," Cat tells MacInerny so she'll let the three of us break together. "She's a genius on that cash register."

Shockingly, for once in her life, MacInerny says yes. So I have to spend my break on the roof with Cat and Elise, eating mocha chip cupcakes from Sam's Diner and toasting the Statue of Liberty with ginger ale.

Not that I'm complaining too much.

"You're going to miss us like crazy, you know you will," Cat tells Elise, refilling our tall plastic glasses with Schweppes. "You'll be dribbling past half-court and it'll just hit you: *Man*, I miss hanging with Cat and Diana. I wonder what those girls are up to right now."

"I won't have to wonder, I'll *know*," Elise grins. "Besides, I'll be back in three months."

"Three cold, empty months," says Cat. "Cheers."

We clack our plastic glasses together. "It won't be the same here without you," I say to Elise, and it's true.

"If you miss me that much, come to one of our games," says Elise. She balls up her cupcake wrapper and tosses it into the Dumpster below. "Three-pointer!"

Cat keeps cracking jokes as we climb down the ladder and get back to work, but all I can think is *When am I going to pick up that vest?* I can't leave the cleaners without getting caught, and I can't send anyone else, since the soundstage location's top secret. The only solution I can come up with is to call Nelson's cell from the fur storage vault.

"I wondered when I would be hearing from you," he says as soon as he answers.

I'm almost afraid to ask, but I have to find out. "Did you have time to sew me a vest?"

"Better than the original. Wait till you see it."

I'm totally thrilled. "Nelson, you rule the planet!"

"I do," he says. "True fact. Want me to ask Sound Booth Junior to bring it?"

"Will. His name's Will."

"Yeah? And is he your boyfriend?"

"We're *friends*," I say, blushing the color of Nelson's pincushion.

"Uh-huh. That's what they all say," says Nelson.

I'm not going to go there. So Nelson and I make arrangements for Will to meet me outside the employee entrance at five forty-five. I thank Nelson about sixty more times and hang up.

Fifteen minutes before closing time, I tell MacInerny I have to go to the bathroom, and scurry back to the employee entrance. Chris is mopping the hall where somebody spilled a big splat of coffee. I don't want him to see me get a package from Will, so I move toward the soda machine instead of the door. I stand in front of it, staring at every selection, pretending that I just can't make up my mind.

"Try Eeny Meeny," Chris suggests. "It doesn't make much of a difference. It all tastes like sugar."

"Yes, but there's Coke moods and Sprite moods. I can't decide which one I'm in," I say. I count out my change really slowly, then go through the motions of starting to choose, and then changing my mind.

Finally, Chris is done mopping up the spill. "Root beer," he says. "You want root beer. Trust me on this one." As soon as he pushes his mop bucket into the men's room, I go straight to the door.

Will's standing outside in a Bob Marley hoodie. He hands me a package wrapped up in white dressmaker's tissue. The logo, drawn on with a Sharpie, says NELSON COUTURE. I fold back the paper, and there is the world's coolest vest! It looks just like the real one, except for the stitching around the buttonholes. Leave it to Nelson to make something great even better. Nelson is my hero.

Well, one of my heroes.

"Thank you *so* much," I tell Will.

"Any time. You excited?"

I nod. "So excited I think I might faint."

"Nah. You'll be fine," says Will.

"You think?" He's probably right — I'm always more nervous *before* I audition than when I have something to do. I bet it's like that when he plays the bass.

"What is it you and Jess always say? Break a legume?"

I can't believe he remembered that! I feel like hugging him, but I don't want to weird him out. "Right! Break a lunch, break a leprechaun. Any word that starts with *L*, except leg. That's too normal."

"Okay." Will pauses for what seems like ages, then says, "Break a later."

Dad pulls up in front of Masala. The restaurant is painted a deep golden orange, like a pumpkin that's gone to a tanning booth. Sara's family lives right upstairs. Dad and I walk around to the side door and press on the doorbell next to the stairs.

"It's Diana," I say into the intercom.

"Come on up!" says a breathless voice, and the door buzzes open.

I rush up the staircase, hoping she's ready. You cannot *ever* be late to auditions. It shows unprofessional work habits.

Sara is standing in the center of the living room, while her grandmother finishes draping her in yards of vivid pink sari silk. I stare at her. "Wow!"

"Is it too much?" asks Sara.

"You look fantastic!" She really does, too. I knew Sara was cute, but I never realized she was so beautiful. Her eyes are lined and her thick black hair shines. In these rich tones of pink with gold accents, she looks like a movie star.

"You said they were looking for somebody Bollywood. I figured I'd give them the whole nine yards. Literally." She lifts up the edge of her sari, then twirls to give her grandmother a kiss. "Thank you, Naani."

I feel very plain by comparison, standing there in my unzipped jacket, black jeans, and Converses. And then I remind myself I have the Magic Vest right in my backpack. That's all the good luck charm I need.

Chapter Five

Dad drives us straight to the Holiday Inn. There's a sign in the lobby advertising a teachers' convention, but nothing about Tasha Kane — or a lip gloss commercial.

As we head toward the desk, one of those twinkle-lit elevators inside a clear tube comes down to the lobby. The door opens wide, and out spills a group of five teenage girls. It's easy to guess where they're coming from. Three of them look Indian, and one is an out-and-out ballerina with scrunched-up leg warmers and feet at right angles. She glances at Sara's sari and stifles a smirk.

Now I have something new to worry about: Will everybody but us be trained dancers? These girls look older, too, like they're in high school and have driver's licenses. We might be totally out of our league.

"Lip gloss commercial?" the desk clerk asks us, sounding so bored that it's obvious she has no clue what these auditions are really for. I bet she's a Tasha Kane fan, and she'd go berserk if she knew.

Sara and I both nod, and she points toward the same elevator. "Conference suite B, second floor."

"I *love* these elevators!" Sara gushes. "It's like a theme park!"

Dad steps in right behind us. Somehow it didn't occur to me he would come *with* us. How am I going to put on my vest? If he sees it, he'll think I got hold of Nikki's. Again.

My palms start to sweat and I force myself to take deep breaths. *You can do it*, I tell myself as the elevator swoops up through its tube. *It'll all work out.*

Luckily, there's a waiting lounge right outside ballroom B. A casting assistant finds our names on a clipboard, and hands us some forms to fill out. As we're signing them, he tells Dad to take a seat.

"How long is this likely to take?" Dad asks, frowning a bit.

The assistant just shrugs. "Till they're done."

Dad looks at us and says, "Good luck." I wince — doesn't he know the old stage superstition that you never *say* that? — but it's too late.

"Thanks," I tell him, and Sara echoes, "Thanks, Mr. Donato." He crosses the lounge and sits down with what must be a group of stage mothers.

"May I use the ladies' room?" I ask the assistant.

"Right inside," he says. Perfect!

We go into a room lined with folding chairs, where several more girls our age are already waiting. Sara and I head straight for the bathroom, where I slip on my bangles and belt, check my hair in the mirror, add a quick brush of lip gloss, and — last but not least — put on The Vest. Nelson's copy is *perfect*. The buttons he used are a tiny bit different, but that stitching he added makes them look just as cute as the originals. He's tailored it to my measurements, too, so it fits even better than Nikki's.

Sara gasps. "That is *so* adorable! Where did you get it?"

I tell her the truth. "From a friend."

"You look fabulous."

"No, *you* look fabulous."

"*You* look rock 'n' roll," Sara says.

"We're both rock 'n' roll fabulous. Let's not be late."

We rush back out and sit with the other girls. They're all sizes and shapes, which is really cool — the video makers must be going for a "real girls" look instead of casting cookie-cutter teen models. Several of the other girls look as if they might be Indian, but Sara's the only one wearing a sari.

I turn my head slowly, not wanting to make it too obvious that I'm counting heads. There are fourteen of us. No one stares, but we all check each other out: This is, after all, the competition. Also, I want to find out what teen actresses wear to a callback. I wonder if any of these other girls are newbies, or if they're all seasoned pros who do this kind of thing all the time. It's hard to imagine how anyone could be more excited than I am.

Except maybe Sara. She keeps grabbing my arm and whispering, "Can you *believe* this?" I've already told her she's not going to meet Tasha Kane — no way is the star going to come to an extras audition — but she's craning her neck all over the place, as if Tasha might be hiding behind one of the panels dividing the conference suite, or inside a potted plant.

An Asian woman holding a clipboard comes out and surveys us. It's Rachel, Tasha's assistant! Somehow recognizing her makes this feel even more real. I remember standing in the costume shop beside her and Tasha while Nelson snapped my picture, and my stomach does a flip-flop. I wish I'd skipped out on that cupcake from Sam's Diner.

"Last group of the day," Rachel says, sounding much more relieved than she probably should. How many groups have they already seen? There could be dozens of girls trying out, if not hundreds. My hopes start to sink, but I remind myself it's an adventure no matter what happens. "Follow me."

We all pick up our bags and trail after her into a larger room. The first thing I see is a video camera and two crew members. My heart starts to thump like a drum machine.

A man with trendy rectangular glasses and hair buzzed into a patterned fade gets up from his director's chair. He's wearing a black T-shirt, jeans, and hip two-tone shoes that remind me of some vintage car.

"Right, then," he says in an English accent, and I realize it's the director! "There's no good or bad here, you're all sensational. I'm looking for just the right mix to be working with Tasha. Line up and let me see those gorgeous faces."

We arrange ourselves into a line. A couple of confident types claim the center, and Sara and I are the last on the right.

The director moves slowly along the line, looking closely at each of the girls. He asks a few to step forward. Sometimes he and Tasha's assistant talk together, their heads close. It reminds me a little of *Project Runway*. Are the ones who've been asked to step forward going to be *in* or *out*?

Finally he gets to our end of the line. He looks right at Sara, smiles, and asks her to step forward. My heart's pounding out of control as he looks at me. I try to meet his eyes through his glasses, projecting *Say yes!* but he doesn't show any response. In fact, he turns away, moving back toward the center. Then I see Rachel touching his arm, angling her head toward my vest. The director turns back to look over his shoulder. He looks from my face to the vest and back, nods and says, "Step forward, please."

I take a big step and stand right next to Sara. Whether we're both in or out, we'll share the same fate. I'm tempted to squeeze her hand, but it seems unprofessional.

"Girls in the front," the director says, and I hold my breath, just like a *Runway* contestant. "I would like you to stay."

Sara gasps out a helium squeak. I know just how she feels — I'm as amazed as she is. The director is thanking the rest of the girls, but I'm too psyched to take in his words. We're still in the running!

But as the other girls gather their things and go out, shoulders slumping, I feel a twinge of pity. I would be so disappointed if I had to leave now. The director picked Sara as soon as he saw her, but I can't help wondering what would have happened if Rachel had not tapped his arm. He was already turning away, so he probably wouldn't have picked me.

I guess I got lucky, but why? Did I make it into this final cut because Rachel said Tasha liked *me*, or my vest? Maybe I just happened to have the right outfit at the right time. But I don't want to think about that now — I need all my confidence. Whatever the reason, I'm in, and I'm going to give it my very best shot.

There are six of us left. The director, whose name is Keith, tells us a little about the video concept. The song is called "Have U Heard?" Tasha plays a girl who gets gossiped about everywhere she goes. The scene we're trying out for takes place in a classroom, with a row of girls turning to whisper a secret from one to the next. Then there's a second setup with the same gossip girls at a row of school lockers.

"So we're going to put you all on tape," Keith says. My heartbeat goes haywire. On tape? As in, *screen test*?

"Here's the drill," Keith goes on. "I want you to walk on nice and casual — think schoolgirls, not runway — and hit these taped marks on the floor. I don't want to be seeing the top of your head as you dip down to find them, so you've got to use your sixth sense, third eye, and all that. Got it?"

We all nod. "Then you're going to look right into the camera and tell it your name, as if it's a person. Give me your left profile, right profile, an extra-nice smile, and walk off to the right. Rachel?"

Rachel walks forward, eyes level, and stops with her toes on the twin strips of blue duct tape. "Rachel Wu," she says with straightforward confidence. She turns left, then right, smiles brightly, and walks off to the opposite side.

"Simple, right?" says Keith. "Okay, line up."

We line up at the spot where Rachel began her walk. Sara and I are at the end again, but that's good: It'll give us a chance to watch everyone else. Keith cues the camera crew, and yes, he really does say, "Action."

I'm in heaven.

The first girl out is tall and striking with a mane of dark hair. She hits her marks like a pro, but she must have missed Keith's "not runway," because she gives plenty of attitude. The next girl steps right over the marks, which might not be so bad if she didn't say, "Oops." I guess we're not the only amateurs in this batch.

The third girl is fine, but not very sparkly. The fourth reminds me a little of Cat — petite, with great eyes and a big personality. She pronounces her name — Izzy Santoro — with a sassy accent, snaps her turns left and right, and ends with a mischievous grin. She's the first one I would cast.

Sara's up next. I hold my breath, almost more nervous for her than I am for myself. But if she's feeling flustered, she covers it well. She's used to high pressure from spelling bees and band competitions. The sari silk rustles gracefully as she walks toward the blue strips on the floor, touching them both with her toes as if she's been hitting marks all her life. She's a natural!

Well, sort of. She looks at the camera and says, "Sahira Pra . . . um, Parvati." She turns left and right, smiles a radiant smile, and walks off just as gracefully. At least she didn't let her stumble throw her, unlike the poor Oops Girl, who looks as though she's going to cry.

I'm up next. *Last but not least*, I tell myself. This is my chance to show Keith that I'm a real actress, not just a girl who got lucky with wardrobe. My heart's pounding out of control.

I take a deep breath, remembering what Ms. Wyant said about coming onstage. You make the space yours from the moment you enter; you fill it up with your bright energy. I walk to the center, trying to sense the tape strips with my peripheral vision. I'm not sure I'm right on the mark, but I take another note from Ms. Wyant and act *as if.* I just *assume* I'm in the right place, say my name, and make my turns. As I'm starting to smile on cue, I remember I'm here to audition for *Tasha Kane* — that Tasha *invited* me — and a giant grin bursts across my face. No sense memory needed!

"Great job," says Keith. He glances at Oops Girl, as if he's considering letting her go on the spot, but decides to be kind and not single her out. "We've just got one more thing to put on tape. I'm going to bring you back out on the floor and treat you to a little sneak preview of 'Have U Heard?'"

There's a stir of excitement around the room. Sara gasps out loud, and Izzy says, "*Sick!*"

"So we're going to roll tape and just ask you to let loose. It's not about dance steps — we've already cast backup dancers. I just want to see how you *move*. So no nerves. Just have fun and rock out with it. Show me your joy."

Well, I can do *that*!

The song pulses on and we all dance like crazy. It's the same irresistible tune Tasha was singing when Will took me into the sound booth. The song is so catchy it's all I can do not to sing along.

I look at the other five girls as I dance. Izzy's got great hip-hop style — she's filled with energy and completely alive. But Sara's the best in the room. She manages to channel the Indian dance moves and graceful hand gestures she's learned from her grandmother into a pop rhythm and I can't take my eyes off her. She smiles right at me as she dances, and I grin back. Even if nothing else happens, I'll always remember this moment. If Keith and Rachel are looking for joy, here it is.

When the song ends, we all applaud, jumping and squealing like we're at a concert. "Yes!" Keith says. "That is the stuff!"

Even the cameraman's grinning. This song's going to be a huge hit.

"Right, listen up," Keith says, getting more serious. "We're going to go over today's tapes with Tasha and her producers. If you're in, you'll be hearing from Rachel on Tuesday. Be cool and stay happy."

Sara and I are both over the moon. We practically float out to the lobby, where I see Dad, talking to three of the women he's sitting with. It isn't until he stands up to greet me that I suddenly realize: *I'm wearing a copy of Nikki Felter's vest!*

In a panic, I dodge behind Sara, hoping her loosely draped sari will hide me till I pull my jacket on over the vest. "Don't move," I hiss.

"What?" she says, turning. "Why not?"

"Tell you later," I say, getting caught with one arm in the sleeve. "Help me, quick!"

Looking mystified, Sara helps me straighten my jacket and I zip it up in the nick of time, just as Dad arrives next to us. He's tucking a small stack of Cinderella Cleaners business cards back into his wallet and looks very pleased.

"I met some new customers. Very nice people." He looks at us both. "Are you done? Some of the girls came out ages ago."

"They got typed out," I say, proud that I know the term. Not for the first time, I'm grateful Ms. Wyant has taught us so much.

"We got to stay and dance!" Sara says, her eyes shining.

"Your dancing was *great*!" I tell Sara.

"Yeah, well, you can pronounce your *name*!"

"Oh, come on, it was nothing!"

"My tongue just got stupid," Sara moans. "That's how I glitched in the spelling bee, too. On a word I knew!"

"Well, you totally nailed it."

"No, *you* nailed it."

"Consider it nailed," says Dad. He puts his hands on our shoulders and herds us both toward the down elevator, saying, "It's past dinnertime."

We drop Sara off right in front of Masala. "That was completely superb," she says, giving me a big hug. "Thank you, Mr. Donato."

Dad waits till she's safely inside. The restaurant is lit up with hanging lanterns that cast shadows over the walls. Is it my imagination, or can I smell curry spices right through the car window? I'm suddenly starved.

It's not far to our house, but Dad wants to hear what the audition was like. As we pull into the driveway, I remind him he can't breathe a word around Ashley and Brynna.

He nods. "Fay bought them two Tasha Kane T-shirts. I hope you get a chance to have them autographed."

"Me, too!" I say fervently.

"Or we could ask Nelson to do us a favor," Dad says.

I shift in my seat, so aware of the favor from Nelson I've got hidden under my jacket that I have the feeling the vest must be giving off light, like a glow stick. The coat closet's right in the hall, in full view of the kitchen. I can't take my jacket off there without everyone seeing the vest. I better go straight to my room.

But when we come in through the kitchen door, Fay is at the stove, already ladling chili into two bowls. There's corn bread and salad on one end of the table, with two plates for us.

"We already ate," she announces. "The girls have a project."

Dad hangs up his jacket. I don't.

"What kind of a project?" I ask, pretending to be so interested that it pulls me right into the living room, where both twins are sprawled on the couch.

"We have to write Spooky poems," Brynna says.

"What's a Spooky poem?"

Brynna picks up her worksheet and shows me. The capital letters along the left edge spell out the word **SPOOKY**, and she's adding words in with a pencil.

> **S**limy snakes
> **P**opcorn popping
> **O**ld witch with an
> **O**wl on her hat!
> **K**
> **Y**

I miss having homework assignments like this. "That's really good," I say. "I like how you made the two *O*'s the same sentence."

"Yeah, but nothing begins with a *K*," Brynna whines. "What did you do, Ashley?"

"Don't *copy*!" says Ashley, covering her poem with her hand.

"What about *Kick*?" I suggest. Brynna giggles and Ashley glares at me.

"How come you've still got your coat on?"

"It's cold out," I say. Is she psychic, or what?

"But you're not out. You're in," she says, folding her arms.

"I got chilled," I say, gritting my teeth as I head for the stairs.

"Where are you going?" Fay demands. "I just served your dinner."

Oh, help. Now she's in on it, too!

"Bathroom," I say. Try and argue with *that*, I think as I charge upstairs, pulling the bathroom door shut. I unzip the jacket and look at myself in the mirror. This vest is totally fabulous. I owe Nelson, big-time. I take it off, carefully folding it back in the dressmaker's tissue and stashing it inside my backpack. So far, so good.

I do all the dishes from dinner and manage to get through some of my homework, though not without stopping about fifty times to replay the audition in my head. I picture Keith telling us, "Show me your joy," and switching the song on. I feel the same rush of adrenaline every time.

But how did I actually *do*? Is there any chance in the world I might really get cast? I can't even imagine how great that would be. I would be walking on air.

Make that *dancing*.

I flop down on my back, gazing up at my ceiling collage of old *Playbill*s. For a moment, I almost wish it was the twins' Tasha Kane shrine instead. Then I look at *The Lion King* program, remembering when I saw that show with my mother. I wish I could tell her about my audition. She used to sit right on the edge of this bed, reading books to me. Sometimes she'd lie down on the bedspread, her head on the pillow next to mine, telling me stories and asking for mine. "What was the best thing that happened today?" she would ask, and I'd get to relive it all over again. Fay didn't even ask how the audition went. I guess she just assumes that I don't have a prayer.

The phone rings on the nightstand right next to my head, and I jump. It's Jess, of course. Someone else who I wish I could tell.

But as usual, Jess wants to talk about Jason, and Jason, and did I mention Jason? Apparently, 4-J has posted new photos on Facebook and I *have* to see them, they're sooo great.

I feel a wave of impatience. It isn't that I'm not happy for Jess, but she's, like, *obsessed* with this guy. What if I broke my vow of silence and told her I'd had an audition today, a professional screen test for Tasha Kane? Would she even care? It's as if my best friend, the only person I know who loves acting as much as I do, who can always make me laugh, has suddenly morphed into Crush Girl.

"Are you listening?" says Jess, and I realize I wasn't.

"Sorry," I tell her. "Just spaced out."

"I hope I'm not boring you," Jess says sarcastically. The truth is, she's been kind of sharp with me ever since I lost her phone at the Foreman Academy. Even though I risked my neck getting it back for her, and she's got a boy who keeps calling her on it. And texting her. And sending photos.

"Of course not," I say, feeling instantly guilty. "Tell me everything."

That's all Jess needs to hear. She talks on and on, and I do my best imitation of listening attentively, when all the while I'm dying to tell her what happened to *me* today.

Chapter Six

Sunday morning is brunch time at my house. Dad's bring-ing the twins to LaToria's Bakery to pick out something special. He asks whether I'd like to join them. Fay's having her beauty rest. I'm tempted — I love the sweet smells of the pastries and breads wafting out of the ovens — but it's even more tempting to stay in pajamas all morning, so I tell him no.

The moment Dad backs his car out of the driveway, the phone rings. I reach for it, sighing. I wonder what Jason's done now.

But it's not Jess, it's Sara. My mood brightens instantly. Finally, someone I can share my excitement with!

"Could you sleep at all?" I ask her.

"Barely," says Sara. "Could you?"

"I dreamed about dancing. I had that song stuck in my head all night long."

"Me, too!" She wants to hear the whole story again about how I met Tasha at the soundstage — every detail of what she was wearing, what she said to me, what the place looked like, right down to the lights in the sound booth. I tell her, savoring every detail.

"It's so weird. If Will hadn't gone to get milk shakes from Sam's at exactly that moment, none of this would have happened at all," I finish.

"I can't believe Will kept it secret so long," Sara says. "Most guys will show off and brag about *nothing*."

"I know, right?" That *is* really cool, I think. Kudos for Will.

"Will's nice," Sara says, as if she were reading my thoughts. "He sits right behind me in band."

"What does he play in the band?" I ask, suddenly super-curious about anything having to do with Will Carson.

"The euphonium."

"*What?*" I say, laughing.

"It's like a baritone horn, or a miniature tuba," says Sara. "Your basic oom-pah-pah."

I can't help picturing Will in a feathered felt hat and those weird German shorts with embroidered suspenders. Would he still be wearing a rock 'n' roll T-shirt? The thought makes me smile.

Monday finally comes, and Jess is on time for a change. The leaves on the ground have a light rime of frost, and our breath comes in puffs. Kids are just starting to climb off their yellow buses as we cross the parking lot. Suddenly, Jess stops in her tracks and reaches into her pocket, where her phone is on VIBRATE.

"It's *him*!" she exclaims.

I don't have to ask who she means.

Jess gasps and giggles. "Check this out!" She hands me her red phone, which displays a text message:

gd morning!

Right above it is a picture of sleepy-eyed Jason — who is pretty cute, I have to admit — with his chin almost touching the rim of a huge bowl of cereal and blueberries.

"Isn't that *great*?" exclaims Jess, and without waiting for me to answer, she grabs back her phone and starts texting with both her thumbs.

Maybe she and Jason really are *going out*.

As I stand waiting for her to finish, I spot Will coming down the steps of his bus, with a big leather instrument case. Must be his oom-pah-pah-phonium, I think, smiling. Will notices me and smiles back, and I realize my ears have become warm, and my cheeks feel like I've got a fever.

Is this crush thing *catching*?

It must be, because I'm totally disappointed when Will goes to the band room again during lunch. Sara's talking nonstop about her favorite singers, and acting so I've-got-a-secret in front of Amelia that I have to step on her foot under the cafeteria table, bringing my index finger up to my lips as if I were brushing a crumb away, not saying, "Shh!"

"Riiiight," Sara says, sounding even more suspect as she changes the subject too fast. Luckily, Jess is still showing Amelia the photo of J-4 with his bowl of cornflakes, so it goes right over their heads.

I don't see Will again till we meet in the doorway of our English classroom. I dip my head, hoping he won't notice me turning a nice autumn red, like an apple.

Just in case things aren't already awkward enough, our English teacher, Mr. Amtzis, has decided we should read *Romeo and Juliet* out loud, to "discover the poetry." Some kids have been complaining it's too hard to read Shakespeare's language.

"You gotta look up every word," grumbles Zane Graf, who used to date Kayleigh Carell. "It makes zero sense."

"Not if you listen," says Mr. Amtzis. He sits on the edge of his desk. "Think about hearing a song for the first time. You might not catch every last word, but you get the *intention*. The meaning comes through the singer's emotion as well as the words. Plays are meant to be *heard*."

He looks at the class. "Any volunteers to read Juliet?"

Acting! My hand goes right up. So does Kayleigh's. Ever since she played Emily Webb in *Our Town*, she's been acting as if she's the star of stage, screen, and school. It's completely obnoxious.

"And I'll need a Romeo." None of the boys raises his hand except Ethan, who's been Kayleigh's boyfriend since they were in *Our Town* together and she switched over from Zane to her costar. She gives Ethan a smug little isn't-this-perfect smile, as if they've already been cast in the leads.

"Let's hear Diana," says Mr. Amtzis. Kayleigh lets out an angry snort under her breath, and Zane looks really pleased. "Ethan, you played Mercutio last time we read. How about . . . Mr. Carson?"

Will, who's been doodling band logos all over his notebook, looks up self-consciously.

"You know a bit about songs, I suspect," Mr. Amtzis says drily. "So let's hear your Romeo. Sara, will you read the Nurse?"

Kayleigh groans rudely. I wish I could tell her that Sara and I tried out for a Tasha Kane video on Friday. She'd be bright green with envy. But Kayleigh's the least of my worries. The Nurse being in this scene means it must be . . .

"The balcony scene," says Mr. Amtzis.

I gulp.

The balcony scene is the most famous love scene in history. *Tell me I don't have to read this out loud with Will!* I will shrivel and die of embarrassment.

Will looks at least as uncomfortable as I do as our teacher brings him up to the front of the classroom and asks me to stand on a chair by the window.

"It's night and the moon's out. You just came home from a dance where you met this great boy, and you're dreaming about him," he tells me. I try to conjure up Adam Kessler in *Angel*, but it's hard for some reason when I'm looking at Will.

Mr. Amtzis turns toward Will. "You can't think of anything else except *her*. Forget the words. Just make it sing."

Looking as if he'd like to sink right through the floor, Will lowers his head and starts rushing through Romeo's opening speech. "But soft, what light through yonder window breaks?" he drones. Clearly his heart isn't in this; he just wants to get it over with so he can sit down.

But after he's run through about half the speech at radio-deejay speed, the words start to make more sense. "It is my lady. O it is my love!" he reads. "O that she knew she were!"

Mr. Amtzis is right — it does sound a bit like a pop song, like a lyric he's singing to someone he loves from afar.

That would be . . . *me*.

It's not too difficult to get into character.

"O Romeo, Romeo, wherefore art thou Romeo?" I start, and the famous line raises a giggle or two from the class.

But Juliet doesn't know her lines are famous — she's just a teenage girl by herself in her room, trying to work out her problems by moonlight. She's crushing on a guy who she knows is off-limits.

Hello? Is there any girl living who doesn't know just how that feels?

We keep reading. Will never looks up from his book. Either he's too shy or he doesn't know the trick of skimming a phrase at a glance so you can make eye contact. Probably both. But as our two characters speak to each other, it sounds more and more like Will gets what Romeo's saying.

That's not true of Sara, who misses every one of her cues, and then says, "Oh! Sorry!" before she reads her line. She reminds me of Oops Girl.

But that barely matters at all. The poetry pulls me along like a river, and so does the look on Will's face as he starts really listening. By the time I get to Juliet's "Parting is such sweet sorrow, That I shall say good night till it be morrow," I have no clue if I'm acting or telling the truth.

Cinderella Cleaners seems five times as busy as usual. The weather dipped down below freezing last night, so people are pulling out last winter's parkas and bringing them in to be cleaned. I'm in and out of the fur storage locker for pickups all afternoon long, and the weight of the coats makes my arms ache.

We're also getting in more special orders for Halloween, which reminds me that Jess and I still haven't settled on our costumes. I stop by the No Pickup rack, our in-house thrift shop, to see if there's anything new and inspiring. I'm checking out a spangled pink gown when Cat comes back to get me.

"*Nice*. Very Eighties Revival," she says. "There's a customer at the counter asking to see you."

My heart nearly stops. It must be Nikki Felter, or even worse, her mother!

"What does she look like?" I ask Cat as we walk toward the customer counter.

"Dark hair and hip glasses. She looks about your age." So it must be Nikki. "She's with a *cute* boy. Total Hollister model."

Oh, perfect. Not only is this penthouse-apartment princess going to get in my face in front of my father and Miss MacInerny, but she's brought her boyfriend to watch. Is this some new reality series?

But I can't afford to be snarky. Dad's told me how much we need Mrs. Felter's catering business, and I will apologize fifty times plus if that's what it takes.

Cat and I push through the double doors to the customer section, and there at the counter are Jason and Annika from the Foreman Academy! I can't believe my eyes. "Wow, you guys! You came to surprise me at *work*?"

Annika holds up a dry-cleaner bag. "I came to pick up my school uniform. Paint stains gone, poof. It's like magic."

"And I came along for the ride," Jason says.

"As in, he knows the guy with the car," teases Annika.

"My roommate's big brother," says Jason. "I've got *connections*, you get what I'm saying?"

I laugh and say, "Got it." Miss MacInerny is glaring at us.

"So we're going to see you this Friday, right?" Annika asks.

"That sounds so fun," I say, suddenly realizing that I completely forgot to ask Dad or Fay if I could go to the movies with Jess Friday night. I change the subject fast. "So what happened when Brooke figured out she was down to one cell phone?" When I was disguised in the Foreman

Academy uniform Annika's holding, I stole back Jess's phone from the mean girl who'd stolen it at the dance.

"Brooke went ballistic," says Annika happily. "She told everyone in the dorm she was going to call campus security."

"Until Annika told her she couldn't exactly report that something she'd stolen was missing," says Jason. "That shut her up."

I can see MacInerny getting ready to speak, so I beat her to it by saying, "I've got to get back to work, you guys. See you both soon."

"Friday," says Annika. "Very soon."

"Oh." Jason reaches into his pocket and takes out a CD in a paper sleeve. "Could you give this to Jess? It's a mix CD I burned for her."

"That is so cool!" I tell him. "Of course."

"See you Friday," he says with a grin.

As I'm putting the CD into my backpack, I can't help wondering what songs Jason put in the mix, and whether he knows about her Jonas Brothers fixation. In the next instant, I'm wondering what songs Will might put on a mix for me. Not that he'd ever do anything like that, I think, zipping up my pack. Jess is so lucky.

The afternoon drags. Elise and Nelson are gone, and Cat is still supervising Lara up front, so there's no one to talk to. The thing about jobs is the people you work with make all the difference. The same tasks that fly by when you're joking around with your buddies seem endless when you're on your own.

Especially when you're counting the hours till your whole life might change. Tomorrow is Tuesday, when Keith told us they'd be calling the girls who've been cast. *I wonder how Sara is doing,* I think as I go to the fur storage locker to fetch a customer's coat. She must be about to jump out of her skin with suspense. Not for the first time, I wish my life had a FAST FORWARD button.

Closing time comes at last, and I hang up my smock and walk through the now-quiet workroom to Dad's office. He's finishing up a phone call with his accountant. Dad's back is to me, and I overhear him say, "Yes, of course we'd save money by letting him go, but the tailoring shop is already backed up."

They must be talking about Nelson! I pause next to the half-open door, straining to hear more.

"Listen, it's anyone's guess if he'll come back or not. . . . Well, we're working on something. I'll let you know when it falls into place. But if he wants this job, it's still his."

I sigh in relief. But *will* Nelson want to come back, or to stay on the fast track? I mean, Cinderella Cleaners is a great place to work, but if you had the choice, wouldn't you rather design clothes for rock stars and hang out with Tasha Kane?

I would!

Chapter Seven

Tuesday morning is like any other, except that the very first thought in my head as I shut off the alarm clock and roll out of bed is, *Did I get the part?* I'm buzzing with anticipation, my stomach in flutters.

Ashley is hogging the bathroom, and I have to pound on the door three times before she says, "I'm coming, *okay?*" in a tone that can only come from a queen bee third grader. Even her twin sister has to wait her turn.

When I come downstairs, Dad is reading his newspaper, calm as a zen master. Fay, in a navy blue pantsuit and cream-colored blouse, bustles around packing PB&Js, apples, and Cheez Doodles into the twins' matching Tasha

Kane lunch boxes. I make myself a big Mexican salad with leftover corn and beans, grated cheddar and salsa, and grab a container of yogurt. As I'm putting my lunch in my backpack, along with the math homework I'm hoping I didn't mess up, I find Jason's CD.

Oops. I forgot all about that.

When I get to the corner where we always meet, I look down the street and see Jess tearing out of her house in a crazy rush as always. Her unbuttoned coat flies out behind her, and with her Mad Hatter top hat, striped muffler, and bouncing red hair, she looks like nobody else in the world. I smile.

"Guess what I've got?" I greet her.

"I hope it's equation sixteen, because I had no *clue*," Jess says, panting a little from her sprint down the block. "Did you get the answer?"

"I think so, but check it with Sara. She's better at math than the teacher." I hold up my arms. "Which pocket?"

"You're supposed to say 'Which *hand*?'" says Jess.

"It won't fit in my hand. Take a guess." Jess points at the left pocket of my vintage peacoat. "Take another guess."

Rolling her eyes, she points at the right, and I pull out the CD.

"What's this?" she says, then sees Jason's note on the paper sleeve. Her eyes get enormous. "This is from — Oh my god! How did you *get* this?"

"He came to the cleaners with Annika yesterday."

"He *did*?" Jess stares at me. "Why didn't you tell me last night?"

Her tone is accusing, and I can see why. We talked on the phone for twenty minutes, at least half that time about Jason, and somehow I didn't remember to tell Jess I'd seen him, or that he had sent her a gift.

I think fast. "Way to spoil a surprise present," I say.

It works. Jess stops glaring at me and looks at the CD. "He made this for me?" she asks happily. "That is so *sweet*!"

It's the last thing she says to me on our whole walk. All the way up the hill and down the school's driveway, she's on her cell phone, telling Jason she can't wait to play his mix, and where is he right now and what did the dining hall serve for breakfast, and anything else that comes into her head. It's as if I'm invisible.

But I don't really mind all that much, because I get to daydream about Tasha and the phone call I'm crossing my fingers and toes I'll get later today.

When we near school, I take my phone out of my backpack, make sure it's on VIBRATE, and stash it inside my jeans pocket. We're not supposed to bring cell phones to class, but there is no way that I'm missing *this* phone call. That's what hall passes were made for.

I wish I knew exactly what time they were planning to call. I'm going to be totally useless all day, and so is Sara. There's nothing harder than waiting to hear about something you really want.

As soon as we get to the school parking lot, I get a strange feeling that something is going on.

Amelia, who's usually very low-key, swoops down on me like a hawk, grinning hugely as she grabs both my shoulders.

"I cannot *believe* you and Sara!" she says. She's speaking in the kind of dramatic whisper that pretty much announces *I'm not supposed to let anyone hear this, okay?* "This is so unbelievably off-the-charts cool! It's amazing!"

"What is?" says Jess, looking from Amelia to me. My stomach lurches.

Too late, Amelia realizes I've been better at keeping a secret from my best friend than her BFF must have been. Sara rushes over to join us, looking worried, like she might have forgotten to mention that Jess doesn't know yet.

Now she thinks of it.

"What's cool?" Jess repeats, with a little more edge. She looks at all three of us.

I feel my skin getting warm. "You weren't supposed to tell *anyone!*" I say to Sara. I can't believe she held on to our secret this long and then blew it. I'm ready to strangle her.

Sara squirms. "I know, I *know,* but I just couldn't stand it any more. And Amelia won't tell."

"She just did," I say angrily.

"No she didn't," snaps Jess. "I don't have a clue what you're talking about. But whatever it is, I wasn't supposed to hear about it. That's pretty obvious." She sounds really hurt.

"Nobody's trying to leave you out, Jess," I tell her anxiously.

"Oh, no? Then why do all three of you know something unbelievably off-the-charts cool and amazing that I don't?"

There's no way around it. I swallow hard. "You have to swear you won't tell anyone," I say, which ticks Jess off even more.

"How long have you known me, Diana? Come on!" she says.

"It's not just us keeping this secret," I whisper. "It's really, really important."

Jess gives me the eye.

"Okay," I say, shooting Sara a how-did-you-get-us-both-into-this? look. "You know that rumor Amelia heard about Tasha Kane shooting a video somewhere around here? Well, she is."

126

Jess crosses her arms over her chest. "What does that have to do with *you*?"

I sigh. "Because Sara and I got to try out as extras."

Jess stares. "Are you kidding? You're kidding me, right?"

Sara and I shake our heads.

"How did that happen?" Jess demands.

"I can't tell you that part," I say. "I'm sorry. I promised I wouldn't." A guilty look flits across Sara's face. Did she tell Amelia the part about Will bringing me to the sound-stage?

"When was this?" asks Jess. I don't like the expression on her face. Her eyebrows look fierce.

"On Friday."

"You've kept this a secret from me for *four days*? When we've talked every night?" Jess's voice sounds tight and scraped, like she might explode any minute.

To my surprise, I'm the one who explodes. "*You've* talked every night! You haven't asked me one single question. It's always all about Jason!" As soon as I blurt it, I wish I could take it back. But it's too late.

127

"Oh, now it comes out," Jess says, looking wounded. "So it's not about keeping this a secret. You didn't tell me the biggest news ever because you're sick of hearing about Jason?"

"Jess —" I start, but she cuts me off.

"I don't know who you are anymore," she says coldly. And my best friend on earth turns her back on me and stomps away.

I wish the blacktop would crack open and swallow me whole. A lump rises in my throat. If I weren't at school, I would burst into tears.

"I am so sorry," says Sara.

"I don't want to hear it," I snap at her. "You did what you did. It's too late for 'I'm sorry.'" And I storm away just like Jess, thinking, *All my friends hate me.*

Feeling friendless would be bad enough by itself, but things get even worse as the day goes along. As I walk through the halls between classes, I get the sense that people are staring at me, even people I don't really know.

My heart starts to pound. Is it my imagination?

By the time I walk into the cafeteria, there's no mistaking that something is up. When Sara meets me at our usual table, looking contrite, I see people's heads swivel and whispers buzz. I hear somebody say, "Tasha Kane."

Oh, no.

I turn to Amelia, demanding, "Did you tell someone else about this?"

"Of course not," she says.

"Then how does the whole cafeteria know?" It couldn't be Jess; Jess still isn't speaking to me. The last thing she'd do is spread rumors that might make me sound like I'm cool. I look from Amelia to Sara.

"Well, I sort of told Elli last night," Sara murmurs. "But I made her promise she wouldn't say anything."

"I told Roxanne after gym," says Amelia. "But she promised, too."

This is beyond awful. The rumor's gone viral.

"How much did you tell them?" I ask. "Did you mention Will and his father?"

They look at each other. "I might have," Sara admits.

"I might have, too," says Amelia.

"How could you do that? That's so not fair!" I'm so upset I don't know what to do with myself. I shove my lunch back in its bag and stand up.

"Where are you going?" asks Sara.

"I have to find Will."

"I don't know what the big deal is," Amelia says. "Everyone thinks you and Sara are awesome. They wish they were you."

Not this minute, they don't. My best friend is furious at me, and the boy I like thinks I'm spreading rumors about something I swore I'd keep secret. Not quite envy material. "Because I *promised* him! That's the big deal!"

"Try the band room," Sara says, looking sheepish.

The band room is down a long hallway behind the stage. Luckily, there are two bathrooms right next to it — the ones we use when we're backstage for school plays — so no one will question me heading that way. I've always enjoyed going in and seeing the shelves full of sheet music and instrument cases, with kettledrums and xylophones sitting right out on the floor. There are a couple of closet-size practice rooms off the main space. Will must be in one of them.

The sound from behind the first door is a high, breathy flute. Not that one. The next room is empty. From the last one I hear a low, blatty brass instrument playing a bass line. It has to be — what was that instrument called again? The euphorium? That can't be right. Baby tuba. Whatever.

I stand right in front of the door, too nervous to knock. What am I going to say to him?

It doesn't matter, I tell myself. You just need to say *something*. I tap on the door and the instrument stops. I hear footsteps come to the door and Will opens it. He's wearing a black Beatles T-shirt today.

"Oh," he says. "Hi." His face is flushed red, I assume from the effort of playing the brass instrument he's holding.

"Is that your . . . um, tuba?"

"It's not really mine. It belongs to the school."

There's an awkward pause. We both know I'm not here to talk about musical instruments. "I just wanted to tell you . . . I've been hearing rumors, you know, about Tasha?"

"Me, too," says Will.

"I didn't start them. I swear."

Will nods. "Okay."

"It was Sara," I say. "She told Amelia, who told someone else, and I guess it just . . . got around. But I didn't tell anyone, honest."

Will shrugs. "You told Sara."

I didn't think of that, but he's right. I volunteered her for the video while we were in the costume shop, not half an hour after Will asked me not to tell anyone.

Now I feel even worse. "I'm really sorry. I didn't know it would get out like this."

"It's okay," says Will. "It's just . . . in my old school, in Santa Fe? Kids were always, like, hitting me up for concert tickets and stuff. I never knew whether they liked me or just wanted favors."

"So when you moved east . . ."

"I figured if nobody knew that my dad's in the music business, I'd know it was . . . you know, for real."

"I'm so, so sorry," I say, feeling awful.

Will shrugs again and looks down at the floor. His bangs flop down over his forehead. "Stuff happens. No biggie, you know?"

I wish I believed him.

And I wish I could tell him that, yes, it's for real.

For the rest of the school day, people are pointing and whispering, or telling me congratulations. But there's nothing to congratulate me about, because I never got a phone call from the casting director. I want to crawl into a hole.

After school, Sara's a nervous wreck, clinging to her cell phone. "When do you think they'll call? Will they call if we *don't* get parts, or just if we do?"

The answer is probably "just if we do." But I don't want to point out that if we haven't heard by now, we must not have been cast. Which would mean that I've hurt my best friend's feelings for nothing. And I'm still mad at Sara for spilling the beans to Amelia. How could she?

I have to admit, I've had happier moments.

I look at the school doors and spot Jess's top hat coming out. Is she going to come over and say good-bye before I get onto the bus to the cleaners as usual, or walk right by as if I don't exist? I don't want to make eye contact — it would be just too awful if I looked right at her and she looked away — but I keep her in my peripheral vision as she approaches the lineup of buses. And all of a sudden the phone in my pocket starts to vibrate.

I jump like a jackrabbit, twisting to grab it. "Hello?" I say breathlessly. Sara and Amelia are staring at me with big eyes.

"Diana?" says the female voice on the other end. "It's Rachel Wu. You've been cast in the video."

"Oh . . . my . . . GOD!" I say so loudly that Jess, passing by, turns to look. Sara and Amelia both gasp. I flash an astonished thumbs-up to them. Jess stops in place.

"We'll be shooting this weekend," Rachel says briskly.

"I have your e-mail address; I'll send you a call sheet with schedule information. Your fee for the two days is six hundred dollars. Congratulations!"

Fee? I didn't even think about that part!

"That's . . . uh, thank you," I stammer. "Thank you so much."

I close my phone and look at my friends in awed disbelief. "I got cast!"

Amelia pumps her fist into the air, saying "YES!" like I just won a soccer match, and Sara jumps up and down. Even Jess looks a little impressed.

"That is so great!" says Sara. "I *told* you you'd get it!" She's trying really hard not to look too disappointed, but I know how much she was hoping she'd be "the Bollywood girl." As my friends babble congratulations and cluster to hug me, I hear a cell phone with a Tasha Kane ringtone. It's Sara's, of course.

I feel my heart jump. Could it be?

Sara flips her phone open, practically screaming, "Hello? Yes, this is Sahira. . . . I *did*?" Her eyes bug out of her head, and she looks as if she might faint from sheer happiness. "I can't believe this!" she keeps saying. "I can't believe it! Thank you. . . . Yes. Thanks, I will. *Thank* you!"

She hangs up and lets out a shriek that can probably be heard ten blocks away. If the tugboats at Port Newark need a new siren, they know who to call. Sara and I hug each other tight.

All over the parking lot, heads turn. Kids gather around us to find out what's going on, and Sara keeps babbling the news, punctuated with "I can't believe it."

It's too late to keep secrets by now, and I can't help feeling glad that Kayleigh and her sidekick Savannah look totally jealous and bent out of shape. Even Jess looks like she might forgive me. She hasn't said anything yet, but she's too close a friend not to share in the thrill.

"And they're *paying* us!" Sara says. "Six hundred dollars!"

"Whoa!" says Amelia. "That's serious money. You two have gone pro!"

Kayleigh tosses her hair, looking evil. It's so satisfying.

"When are you shooting?" asks Ethan, putting his arm around Kayleigh. I wish Will was with him instead. I'm so eager to tell him my news.

"This weekend," I say, and Sara chimes in, "Friday night and all day Saturday."

"Friday night?" Jess stares at me, her smile disappearing. "We've got *plans* on Friday night."

My stomach drops as I remember the movie I'm supposed to be seeing with Jess and Jason and Annika. I don't know what to tell her, but Sara jumps in before I have a chance. "Are you kidding me?" she says in complete disbelief. "We're shooting a rock video with *Tasha Kane*! What could be more important than that?"

"Obviously not me," replies Jess, before turning and storming off.

I close my eyes, sighing. I've seen enough of Jess's hot temper to know she won't be forgiving me anytime soon.

I'm really upset, but I'm also a little bit angry. I just got a role in an honest-to-goodness rock star's video! I should be turning cartwheels, not worrying about my best friend's reaction. Why couldn't Jess just be happy for me? She's already been too mad to speak to me once today. Couldn't she give it a rest? She's got Jason on Friday. She doesn't need me.

I can't think about it for long, though. The school buses let out their two-minute warning honk, which sounds like a cross between Sara shrieking and Will's tuba thing, and I have to scramble to get on the bus that takes me to work.

It's not till I sit down on my bench and stare out the scratched window that it really hits me. I got the part!

I'm supposed to go in through the employee entrance, but I cannot wait to tell Dad. I rush through the front door and push open the door to his office.

Three sober faces look back at me. Dad's at his desk, MacInerny is sitting in a chair beside him, and a bald man I recognize as Dad's accountant, Morris Smilow, is showing them both a spreadsheet full of figures.

"I — I'm so sorry," I stammer, backing up. "I didn't mean to interrupt."

"What is it?" says Dad, who can read my face better than anyone else on the planet. "You've got good news."

"It can wait."

He looks at the others. "I think we could all use some good news, don't you?" Morris nods. I don't dare look at Joyless. I focus on Dad's encouraging smile and blurt, "I got the part!"

"Really?" Dad says. "That's terrific!"

I nod. "And they're paying me! It's a real *job*!" I suddenly realize I'll be able to pay Dad back for Mrs. Felter's gift certificate, all in one swoop, with a whole lot left over. I beam with pride.

"Mazel tov," Morris says as Dad rises and folds me into a bear hug. I smell the familiar mixture of scents on Dad's clothing and feel like a little girl, safe in his arms.

"I'm so proud of you, honey," he says. "Congratulations!"

"I'll tell you the rest of it later," I promise.

He nods and shows me to the door, where he whispers, "Autographs for your sisters, all right? They'll be kissing your hem."

I can't see the twins kissing anyone's hem, but I nod and say, "Sure!" Lara looks up from the cash register, where she's ringing up someone's order. I smile at her as I flip up the hinged counter section, but as soon as I push through the doors to the workroom, my face gets as serious as Dad's.

His words echo inside my head: *I think we could all use some good news.*

What's going on? Has Mrs. Felter withdrawn her Garden State Catering business? Or is there some other disaster that I haven't heard about yet? Does it have something to do with Nelson? As thrilled as I am about my great news, it won't fix the rest of my problems.

Like Jess being mad at me.

Jess doesn't call me that night, for maybe the third or fourth time in our lives. I think about picking the phone up myself, but I'm pretty sure she'd just hang up on me. She was really upset when I lost her cell at the Foreman Academy, but it was nothing like this. That was a simple mistake, one I managed to fix by getting her phone back. This is different. Jess isn't just disappointed in me for leaving her purse in the wrong place. She feels betrayed.

Another thing's different, too. When Jess's cell got stolen, I knew that I'd made a stupid mistake, and I just wanted Jess to forgive me. This time, I'm mad at her, too. There was a really good reason that I didn't tell her about Tasha's video: I made a promise to Will, and I kept my word. It was *Sara* who did the wrong thing, but is Jess mad at Sara? No. Only at me.

I turn out my lights, but I can't get to sleep. I feel like I'm on a roller coaster of emotions: I'm totally thrilled about getting cast in the video, totally worried about Dad and the cleaners, and totally scared that I've blown it big-time with Jess *and* with Will. That's three totals at once. Why does everything have to be so *complicated*?

I sit up in bed, hugging my pillow against my chest. More than anything else, I wish Mom were here. She'd be so proud of me for landing this role, and somehow she'd know what to do about everything else.

The window is open a crack, and a cool breeze rustles the edge of the curtains and lifts my hair. I close my eyes, and it's almost as if I can hear Mom's voice, gentle and soft in my ear. "Just tell the truth," she says, and I open my eyes, feeling better. I know what I have to do.

Chapter Eight

The next morning, I leave for school ten minutes earlier than usual so I can meet Jess at her house. I don't even know whether she wants to see me, but I need to talk.

It's the usual getting-ready chaos at the Munson house. Jess comes to the door in a purple cardigan over a black cami, gray jeans, and bare feet. She gives me a long look that could mean almost anything. But all she says is, "I'm not even close to being ready."

"For a change," says her kid brother, Dash, and Mrs. Munson says to him, "You're not ready, either, so hold your tongue." Dash opens his mouth and grabs hold of his tongue. Typical fifth-grade boy humor.

"Oh, get over yourself," snaps Jess, and I'm so relieved to see her get mad at somebody else that I laugh, even though it's not really that funny. There's a last-minute scramble for socks and shoes — one black flat is in Jess's bedroom, one under the couch with the TV remote — and we finally set off for school.

There's frost spiking the grass, and the air is so cold we can both see our breath. For several minutes those puffs of warm steam are all that come out of our mouths, hovering like empty cartoon bubbles.

"I'm really sorry I'm missing the movie," I say, and at almost the same moment, Jess says, "I'm sorry for losing my temper. I guess I'm just jealous."

Really?

"Well, I'm jealous, too," I blurt out.

Jess stops in her tracks, staring. "Jealous of *me*?"

I nod and confess the truth: that I feel left behind by her having a boy who likes her enough to e-mail her photos and give her surprise presents and ask her to movies. "You're . . . you have a *boyfriend*! You and Jason are *going out*!"

Jess looks at me as if she can't believe what she's hearing. "*You're* in a rock video! You went to the opening of *Angel* and got to dance with Adam Kessler! Your life is so much more exciting than mine, it's ridiculous."

"Really?" I feel kind of silly.

"Yes, really. And not only that — if you weren't so blind, you'd be going out with someone, too."

My mouth drops open. What is she talking about?

Jess says, "I've been trying to tell you forever that Will likes you, but you both keep insisting you're just friends. It's driving me crazy."

I gulp. "*Both?* You mean you talked to Will?"

Jess rolls her eyes skyward. "We're friends. Duh!"

"When? What did he say?" I demand. I'm halfway annoyed she's been talking about me behind my back, and halfway just excited. The excited part is winning.

"Will said you were great."

"He said that? He used the word *great*?"

"Direct quote."

I'm about to ask "Really?" again, but I'm smiling too wide to ask any more questions. "I totally love you, Jess."

"I love you, too, you big doofball." She hasn't called me that since second grade.

"Who are you calling a doofball, you dorkus?"

"You, dork."

"No, *you*, dork."

We're both grinning our ears off. I think we've made up.

I don't have any classes with Will in the morning, and I don't run into him once in the halls. This is a giant relief. I don't really know what I'll say when I see him, or how I should act around him if he does, by some miracle, secretly like me, too. I was self-conscious enough when it was just *me* with a crush. This will be even worse.

Or maybe much better. After all, Jess and Jason went from just-friends to going out, without any speed bumps. Then again, Jason does not have the shy disease. Neither does Jess.

But I can't hide forever. We're in the same English class. Sooner or later I'll have to say *something*.

Oh god. This is terrible. Why can't life come with a script?

Lunch is fantastic. I sit with all three of my besties, and nobody's mad at each other anymore. Sara and I finally get to tell the whole story of how we tried out, and reliving that wonderful day makes me even more thrilled about what's up ahead.

I wonder if any of the other finalists we got to see dance are going to be schoolgirls, and who else got cast — and, of course, what we're going to *wear*! Knowing Nelson Martinez will be sewing my costume makes this part even better.

But thinking of Nelson of course makes me think of Cinderella Cleaners, and Dad, and the money problems I don't dare to ask about. Somehow no matter how sweet things get, there's always something else going on underneath, like the pit in the plum.

And right after lunch, I've got English. I know I'm about to see Will, either at my locker, where I have to pick up my books for my afternoon classes, or when we get to class. I'm feeling incredibly tongue-tied. The roof of my mouth has gone dry, like it does when you eat peanut butter right out of the jar.

I wonder if Will's even heard I got cast. He must have. All day long, kids I barely know have been giving me comments and looks, and Ms. Wyant threw her arms around me and said, "Congratulations, young star!"

While I'm opening my locker, Riley Jackson, who co-starred with me in *My Fair Lady* last year and played the narrator in *Our Town*, slaps me five as he passes and says, "Way to go, pro!"

"Thanks," I say, grinning. I dig through the stack of books inside my locker and pull out my dog-eared copy of *Romeo and Juliet*. When I turn back around, there's Will, holding his.

I remember one of Juliet's lines from the scene we read to each other: "Thou knowest the mask of night is on my face, Else would a maiden blush bepaint my cheek."

My cheek is bepainting, all right. I must be the color of ketchup.

"Hi, Will," I squeak. "Going to English?"

No, he's decided to study Norwegian instead. Why is it that when you get flustered, the first thing you think of to say is always embarrassing?

"Uh-huh," says Will. He's not doing much better than I am. And then he surprises me. "I heard you got cast in the video. That's really cool."

"Yeah, I'm so excited." *Obvious much? Say something else. Just keep talking.* "I can't thank you enough."

Will looks surprised. "What did I do?"

Is he serious? "*Everything*," I blurt.

"You got cast all by yourself," he says. "Tasha really liked you."

"She did?" I can't believe what I'm hearing.

So it wasn't the vest. It was *me*.

Will flashes a self-conscious smile. "Why *wouldn't* she like you? I mean . . ." He trails off, too embarrassed to finish. But he doesn't have to. I know what he means.

Okay. Now I really *am* blushing — and so is he. We can't think of a single thing more to say to each other. We might both stand there getting redder forever, but thank goodness the bell rings.

"We're going to be late," I say, breaking the spell. Will nods gratefully, and we both stumble toward English class, clutching our copies of *Romeo and Juliet*.

The next day, Sara and I are called to the soundstage at four for our first costume fitting. Since we're all teenagers, they've scheduled it after school, but I'll need to leave early from work. Dad's fine with that, and if Joyless isn't, well, she's not fine with *anything*.

The only hard part is not being able to tell Cat why I'm leaving early. Though most of Weehawken Middle School knows Sara and I have been cast in a Tasha Kane video, and even that Will Carson's dad is her sound engineer, the one thing we've managed to keep under wraps is the shooting location. I've heard enough stories of fans mobbing stars on a film set to know it would be a disaster if this information ever leaked out, and Sara feels so guilty about spreading the news around school that she's taking security very seriously. I remind her of what Rachel told me about the audition — that if we tell anyone where the soundstage is, we'll be "right out." She swears up and down that she hasn't told anyone, not even when Amelia begged her.

So even though I know Cat would be crazy excited, I don't breathe a word. Not even when the radio that's always on in the workroom is blasting out one of Tasha's first hits, "This Girl Is Gone," as I'm leaving the building.

Following Ms. Wyant's advice about callbacks, I'm dressed pretty much as I was the first time I met Tasha, except that I've traded the tank top for something more seasonal: a ribbed, striped scoop neck I know will look great with Nelson's Magic Vest. I've added a little more jewelry, too, and my favorite crocheted newsboy hat.

Sara, who meets me in front of the cleaners, looks like a totally different girl. In place of her sari, she's wearing a patterned baby-doll top over leggings, with an orange bomber jacket and side-buckle boots. As we walk the few blocks to the old carpet warehouse, nobody would guess we were anything other than middle school girls on an after-school stroll.

We're deep undercover.

When we get to the warehouse and walk toward the unmarked back door, Sara clutches my hand with excitement. We speak our names into the intercom, and we're buzzed right in. The two hulking security guards I remember are working the counter. The shorter one eyeballs me, frowning. "No entry for *you*, girlfriend."

"What?" I say, starting to panic.

"No friends of Will Carson's back here." He breaks into a broad grin and winks as he passes the metal detector wand over me. "Gotcha. I never forget a face."

"She'll never forget *yours*, that's for sure," says the second guard. "You girls sign in here, all right?" And we do.

Sara is gaping at everything. A production assistant named Alex takes us down the hall to what's called the "green room," where we meet the rest of the schoolgirl extras. There's a freckle-faced redhead who reminds me of Jess, a delicate Vietnamese girl with braces, a plump blonde with a radiant smile, and a leggy African-American girl with long beaded braids. The last to arrive is Izzy Santoro, the live-wire hip-hop dancer who auditioned with Sara and me. She breezes in five minutes late, looks the rest of us over, and says, "Now, this is what I call a *posse*!"

She's right. Even in street clothes, we look terrific together. Alex the P.A. speaks into his headset, "All here. You ready for them?" All of us extras glance at each other. The question hanging over everyone's head — when will we get to see *her*? — goes unspoken, but it's clear we're all dying to meet Tasha Kane.

Alex turns toward us. "Okay, Wardrobe's ready. We're walking."

Wardrobe! That's almost as exciting as meeting the star. In a breathless pack, we parade down the hall to the costume shop, where Ingrid and Nelson are waiting with digital cameras, measuring tapes, and measurement sheets for each character. Most of the other girls are professional actors or models, so they're used to having their measurements taken for costumes, but Sara and I could not be more thrilled. The camera flashes go off again and again.

When it's my turn to be measured, Nelson just grins.

"Yours, I've already got." Then he steps back and looks me over from head to toe. "Though you've gotten taller."

"You think so?" I'm flattered.

Nelson looks down at his handwritten notes. "I have you down at five-five and a half. Let's check it out."

I kick off my Converses and stand against the far wall, where there's a height marking chart. Nelson runs a ruler from the top of my head to the wall and smiles. "Five feet *six*, growing girl." He holds up a hand, slapping me five.

We get back to Cinderella Cleaners forty-five minutes before closing time, so I get a chance to show Sara my world. Cat always loves meeting my friends, and luckily she doesn't ask any questions about where we've been. She falls madly in love with Sara's orange suede jacket, and they spend so long gabbing about where they like to shop that they sound like they've been friends forever.

I show Sara the back room and, like Jess, she thinks it's incredibly fun, especially the fur storage vault and the No Pickup rack.

"If nobody else claims that pink prom gown, it's mine," she says.

I burst out laughing. "I said the same thing!"

"Easy come, easy go." Sara shrugs. "So what kind of outfits do you think they're going to design for the school-girls?" I look over my shoulder, but Cat's at the counter and nobody else is close enough to hear us over the noise of the drying machines.

"Something cute, I hope," I tell her. "Something we'd wear in real life if we had our own costume designer."

"Exactly," Sara says.

I begged Nelson to give me a hint, but all he would say is 'You'll see,' with this Cheshire cat smile."

"Nelson measured me in about two seconds flat," says Sara. "And he's so *funny*!"

"I miss him," I tell her, and that is the truth. Cinderella Cleaners just isn't the same without Nelson. I don't even know what I ought to wish for. It would be wonderful for his designing career if he got to keep working on videos, and it would be selfish for me not to want him to have that chance. Especially when I'm not sure if he'll still have a job to come back to. But I want him back!

I've still got half an hour left to work, so Sara sits down on the bench by the Skittles machine and does homework till closing time. Dad's gotten in touch with her parents and he's going to drop her off at Masala on our way back home.

Of course Dad's the very last person to leave, as he is every night. Sara and I watch as he circles the customer area, whistling a little tune under his breath while he closes out the cash register and turns out the lights one by one.

Before Dad took over the cleaners, when he worked as a house painter, he used to whistle all the time. I haven't heard him do that in a very long time. It makes me a little bit sad.

Masala is lit up with twinkle lights and dangling lanterns in the window. As Dad pulls into a parking space, I'm surprised to spot Fay's SUV across the lot. "What is she doing here?" I ask Dad.

"Oh. I told Fay and the girls to meet us for dinner."

"Really?" Maybe that's why he was whistling. He had a surprise planned.

"That's awesome!" says Sara. "I got to see your after-school job, and now you can see mine."

"Are you working tonight?" I ask.

"No, but you better believe I'll be busing *your* table!" As she opens her door and gets out, I lean over to Dad and whisper, "Can we afford this?"

"Of course!" he says, sounding surprised. "Why would you ask that?"

This isn't the moment to tell him that I've listened in on his conversations with Morris, so I just squeeze his hand and say, "Thank you so much."

Maybe things aren't as bad as I think. Or maybe they are, and Dad's just a really good actor. I guess I'll find out soon enough, but tonight I'm too happy to let my thoughts linger on possible problems.

The meal is terrific. The twins are freaked out by the exotic smells, but Sara sits down at our table and helps them order nonscary food, starting with mango lassi, which are just like thick milk shakes they slurp up through straws.

"This is okay," Brynna says, her upper lip covered with peach-colored foam. Ashley tries a bite of a fried appetizer.

"I like mozzarella sticks better," she grumps, but she eats four.

"Hey!" Brynna tells her. "Don't hog it!"

"I told you you'd like those," says Sara. Her parents keep coming to our table and making a fuss over us, sending dish after dish "on the house."

It's a real celebration. Dad raises his glass in a toast and says, "Here's to our talented daughters." He clinks glasses with Sara's father.

"Hear, hear," says Fay. "*All* of them." I can't tell whether she's just reminding Dad to include *her* two daughters, or trying to make us feel more like one big happy family, instead of two halves that got pasted together.

Dad leans over and gives her a kiss on the cheek. Sometimes when I see him do that, a picture pops into my head of him kissing Mom, and I get such a sharp stab of missing her that I can't breathe. But tonight something's different. Tonight I can watch him kiss Fay and not totally mind.

That's what being happy can do for you. Good to know.

Chapter Nine

By Friday morning, all I can think about is the video shoot. The Tasha Kane T-shirts for Ashley and Brynna are tucked in my backpack. I spent over an hour last night putting together the outfit that I'm going to wear today, but as I'm getting dressed, I change every piece at least twice. I wind up in my favorite black jeans and a turquoise V-neck that looks great with the Magic Vest, plus a wrist full of bangles. I know what I'm wearing won't make a difference to anybody but me — we'll be putting on costumes as soon as we get there — but I've got a whole rain forest of butterflies in my stomach today. If I feel like I look halfway chill, they might settle down a bit.

Accent on "might."

Our call sheet tells us to come to the soundstage at four for Wardrobe and Makeup, with shooting to start at six. That's a whole school day away. Sara and I are beside ourselves with anticipation, and so are our friends. Even Jess. I'm so glad we made up.

At lunch, our usual table has swollen to include Will, Ethan, Kayleigh, and Savannah. Now that Sara and I are the center of so much attention, Kayleigh's started to act like she's all buddy-buddy with me, which is sort of obnoxious and sort of hysterically funny, after the way she's been dissing me ever since sixth grade. Now I'm her best friend from drama club, and our table is suddenly *the* place to sit.

Right. As soon as the video's over, my friends and I will be back in our usual spot on the middle school food chain, not at the bottom, but certainly not at the top. Meanwhile, it's kind of fun getting a sneak peek at Popular World.

Everyone's asking us questions about Tasha Kane. I can see that Will's getting uncomfortable, so I change the subject, turning to Jess. "So what movie are you and Jason going to see tonight?"

Jess shoots a quick glance at Will, who looks down at his hands with a funny expression. "We'll come up with something," she says in a bubbly voice. "I'm sure there'll be something good playing somewhere." This isn't like Jess at all — she's always the one who checks out all the movie schedules online and tells everybody exactly what she wants to see. I guess her excitement about seeing Jason outweighs everything else.

I have to admit that I'm still a teensy bit jealous. Jason was so totally up front about liking Jess, all she had to do was say, *"Yes. Me, too."* Ever since Will and I had that short conversation in front of my locker, he's been even harder to talk to. We used to be regular *friends*, at least. Now it's like we're stuck halfway out on this wobbly bridge between Just Friends and We're Going Out, and neither one of us knows how to take the next step.

When Will gets up from our table and leaves a few minutes before lunch is over, I'm positive it's because he's too self-conscious to walk with me up to our lockers and English class.

Somehow I manage to make it through the post-lunch triathlon: a marathon Silent Will English class, followed by an even longer social studies lecture, and the Guinness World Record for Endless Math. It seems like a month till the bell finally rings. Free at last!

As I leave the school building with Sara, I feel like my whole body's filling with helium, and my feet might lift right off the ground.

Next stop, fame and fortune!

Sara and I sign in at the front desk and meet the other five girls in the green room. Once again, Izzy is last to arrive, in a short leather jacket as red as a summer tomato, acid-wash skinny jeans crisscrossed with two chain-link belts, and a fabulous pair of fringed boots. Whatever Ingrid and Nelson are planning to dress us in, her outfit is going to be hard to top. "Hey, girlfriends," she says, looking at us with an irresistible grin. "Let's get the party started!"

Alex brings us down the hall to the costume shop. I walk through the door and nearly fall over.

Nelson and the rest of the crew have sewn seven vests exactly like mine! Every one is a different color, and every one has a matching electric guitar with a jeweled strap!

We all squeal and exclaim at once, saying "OMG!" and "I love it!" and "Those are outrageous!"

"Hands *off* the guitars, ladies. No rocking out with the props," Nelson says as he passes each of us our costume pieces.

Sara's vest is orange and mine is hot pink. Izzy's is the same vivid red as her jacket, and the others are yellow, green, turquoise, and purple. We each have an outfit in just the right colors to complement our vest and coloring. I can't wait to try mine on.

Izzy looks from the vest in my hands to the dark blue one I'm already wearing. "Hey," she says. "Are you in the loop, or what?"

"Diana *is* the loop," Nelson says, giving me a big wink. "You are looking at Ms. Fashion Forward."

And Ms. Fashion Forward is blushing all over.

"Dressing rooms are right over there," Ingrid says. "Make it quick. Hair and Makeup is waiting for you."

She doesn't need to say anything more. I'm the first girl dressed and the first girl out. When I catch a glimpse of myself in the three-way mirror, I almost start clapping. I look like a rock star!

Nelson comes up behind me, adjusting the buckle on the back of my vest. "Looking good," he says. When I look in the mirror and see his reflection in his black fedora, pop-collared shirt, and suspenders, hovering over my out-fit, it brings such a rush of good memories that I blurt out, "Are you going to come back to Cinderella Cleaners?"

Nelson's eyes scan the mirror to make sure that Ingrid is out of earshot. She's on the far side of the room, fussing with the hem of another girl's outfit. He drops his voice to a confidential near-whisper. "I certainly am. And I'm bring-ing this costume shop with me."

"What do you mean?" I breathe back.

"Where do you think we'll be cleaning those outfits you're wearing? And Ingrid's next gig is a new TV series. She hasn't been pleased with the cleaners she's using. Your dad and I made the producers an offer they couldn't refuse. We hooked them up with a new caterer, too."

"Mrs. Felter from Garden State Catering?" My eyes are enormous.

Nelson nods. "You got it. It all came together this morning."

"Nelson, that is so great. That's amazing!" I feel like throwing my arms around him, but of course I don't. That would not look professional.

Nelson grins. "Great news for me, too. Ingrid's already got a full staff on her show, but you never know when you might need a spare pair of talented hands."

He waves his hands in the air like a magician who's just cast a spell, then taps me on the shoulder and raises his voice so the others can hear. "Okay, you're fabulous. Next?"

We get even more fabulous in Hair and Makeup, which looks like the backstage dressing room of my dreams: mirrors rimmed with lights, comfortable swivel chairs. There's a collage of photos around every mirror, and the radio's cranking Beyoncé. All seven of us are in heaven. Izzy and the curvy blond girl, Kirsten, get so into the music they're practically dancing right in their chairs.

"Sit still or you're gonna have eyeliner racing stripes right down your nose," says the woman who's working on Izzy. They've draped us in beautician's capes to protect our costumes, so our heads seem to float on a sea of blue nylon.

Andrew, who's doing my makeup, has long, graceful hands and intense concentration, like a painter at work on an easel. He doesn't do much, but it's all good. Even when I bring my face right up close to the mirror, I can't see the makeup, but somehow he's sculpted my cheekbones and brought out my eyes so they'll pop for the camera. He back-combs my hair just a little to give it more body, and sprays it with something that smells like vanilla and brings out the shine.

"Do you love it?" he says, and I do.

I trade places with Sara and he goes to work on her. "*Look* at these eyelashes!" Andrew exclaims. "They're to die for!" He picks up tweezers, deftly reshaping the arch of her dark brows. When he's done, Sara looks beautiful — just like herself but more glamorous.

At last we're all primped to perfection. The makeup crew whips off our capes, and we jostle to check ourselves out in the mirrors. As usual, Izzy's the one who says what we're all thinking. "We look *out of control!*" she whoops.

Alex is waiting to escort us down to the set. I thought I was excited before, but at this point I'm pumping out so much adrenaline, I feel like an Olympic sprinter. I almost forget to be nervous. When he opens the door to the stage, my heart rate goes right through the roof.

In front of our eyes is a multiple world. There's a multi-tiered performance stage with a drum set and keyboards already in place, and two standing sets. One's a wide row of school lockers; the second, a partial classroom with a chalkboard and two rows of desks. They both look completely real, except for the fact that they're missing two walls and surrounded by cameras and lights.

But it isn't the sets that blow us away. Keith, the director, is standing dead center, with his arm around somebody we'd all know anywhere.

It's Tasha Kane!

She's wearing a violet tunic over printed leggings, three different gold necklaces, and — this is the part where I nearly faint — black high-top Converses with two different laces, one turquoise, one pink! My signature style, on a rock star! I don't think I've ever been prouder.

"Hey, girls," says Tasha, and something about the way she smiles at us makes me feel right at home. "I'm really looking forward to this one!"

Me, too! And I'm not alone — Sara and all the other girls are beaming. Sara reaches over and squeezes my hand.

"Tasha, you are the *bomb*!" Izzy blurts. She starts clapping and cheering, and the rest of us join her.

"Okay, that's enough of that," Tasha says, but she looks really pleased. "Let's get this thing started."

Keith tells us we're going to be shooting the scene at the hall lockers first. "I'll run through the staging with you in a minute, but let's grab a quick photo op, shall we? You all look sensational."

He lines us all up in front of the lockers, arranging us

by our vest colors so we make a rainbow. "Right, girls, now open your lockers."

We follow instructions, and everyone gasps. Inside are our colored guitars. Keith says, "That's what you'll be doing when we take this shot. The schoolgirls have been trash-talking Tasha all over the classroom" — he points at the other set with the two rows of desks — "and then this incredible song of hers spins you around, and you seven turn into her backup band. Got it?"

We nod. This is going to be awesome!

"Let's do it one time for the still cam, and then we'll rehearse, all right? Get your guitars on."

We all reach into our lockers and strap on our guitars.

"Perfect!" says Tasha, looking at each one of us approvingly. I can't tell if she recognizes me as the girl she pulled into the costume shop — the one with the two-tone laces and borrowed vest. It would be cool to think she remembered my name, or that we had some special connection, but really, her choosing my style for the costumes is more than enough.

Keith arranges us into a half circle, with Tasha front and center. The crew's still photographer starts snapping candid shots, and Keith calls for music. "Let's hear that last instrumental take," he says. "Give these girls something to groove to, okay, Tash?"

As we all stand together and pose for a group portrait, the irresistible hook of Tasha's "Have U Heard?" comes over the big bank of speakers. My heart nearly bursts with joy as she starts singing — only two feet away!

Of course we start dancing. How could we help it? The still photographer twists herself into a pretzel, all elbows and kneecaps as she snaps candid shots. Keith nods, then steps back toward the camera crew, waving his hands as he talks them through moves. One of the cameras is on a big wheeled thing — I think it's called a crane — and two crew members glide along with it, swooping in closer as Tasha prances and sings.

I check out the soundstage, trying to take it all in at once. There are the video cameras, the musicians taking their places on stage. A light snaps on behind what I thought was a big plate-glass mirror, and suddenly I can see the recording crew framed in the sound booth's big window.

And . . .

Right behind them are Will, Jess, Jason, and Annika! They sit together in a row, kicked back in their folding chairs, munching big buckets of popcorn like they're at a multiplex theatre. I almost fall over with shock.

This must be the "we'll think of something" Jess was talking about. Their night at the movies is . . . *us*!

No wonder Will wouldn't look me in the eye or walk to English class with me today! He must have set all this up, and he didn't want me to catch on. This realization sends my heart into the spin cycle.

So does this mean that Will likes me, too? Maybe he really does, and just can't find the words for it. But that's okay — maybe I can. It takes two to be *going out*, right?

As if Will can hear what I'm thinking right through the glass of the sound booth, he smiles and waves.

The video camera tracks past us, and the still camera's flash goes off again and again, like a firework display.

Keith gestures at us to strum our prop guitars and we all move in unison: Tasha Kane's backup band, guest-starring *me*. Jess grins at me, flashing a thumbs-up.

It's hard to imagine how I could be any happier. Everything I love most is right in this room: music, clothes, acting, and — better than anything else I can think of — my friends, old and new.

All right, world, it's official: This totally rocks!

Turn the page for a sneak peek at

Cinderella CLEANERS

#4: Mask Appeal

Jess and I turn onto Underhill Avenue, heading up the long hill toward Weehawken Middle School. My next-door neighbor, Mr. Wheeler, crosses the street with his two tiny papillon dogs. My eyes follow them as Mr. Wheeler walks past the Underhill Deli, and I spot a new poster in the front window. It's bright orange, with a graphic of eyes peering out through a black satin mask. I look up the street and notice the same poster is stapled to every phone pole. Before I have time to react, Jess is pointing to one.

"What's with the mask on that poster?" she asks. "Is someone doing *Phantom*?"

"Not without *us*," I respond, since *Phantom of the Opera* is on my all-time top ten list of shows.

We move closer to look at the poster, which reads:

Dance with the Stars at
HUNGER UNMASKED

"Oh, of course. It's that fund-raiser thing they do every year," Jess says.

I nod. "I heard last year's was great." We keep reading eagerly.

Masquerade Ball to benefit Arts Against Hunger
* Live Music by Dreamcatcher
* Silent Art Auction
* Fleet Feet Dancers
* PLUS Broadway Stars from *Bye Bye Birdie* and —

I gasp out loud. "*Angel*!"

Angel is a new Broadway musical starring my major celebrity crush Adam Kessler. When I first started helping out at the cleaners, I found a pair of opening night tickets left by a customer, and by a series of chances that still feels like magic, I went to *Angel*'s opening night and got to meet Adam, who's even more dreamy in person. Then Jess won a raffle and got to go see the show too. Which is on my all-time top *one* list.

I wonder which "stars" will be at this masquerade ball. Could one be . . . *him*?

As usual, Jess is right on my wavelength. "Do you think Adam Kessler —?" we say at exactly the same time.

Jess laughs and tags my arm, saying, "You owe me a Coke."

My heart does a little flip-flop at the thought of seeing Adam in person again. Not that Jess or I can afford to attend — the tickets cost eighty dollars apiece, with a discount of one hundred fifty dollars per couple. It's all for a good cause, of course, but those aren't eighth grade prices.

"Don't you wish . . ." I start, and Jess says "Yes!" before I even finish my sentence.

"It just looks so *glamorous*," I go on dreamily.

Jess nods. "I wish I could bring Jason." Jason Geissinger is Jess's new crush — I might almost have to say *boyfriend*. Whenever Jess mentions his name, I know I'm going to be in for a monologue. But before she can really get going this time, a gust of wind picks up her top hat, blowing it into a nearby hedge.

Something else blows past us too — a loose poster from the next phone pole. I want that! We pounce like two kittens. Jess scoops up her hat and I grab the poster, and we're both so excited we charge to the top of the hill. Our gym teacher would be proud.

It's not till I go back to my locker for lunch that I remember the Hunger Unmasked poster I saved from the wind. I take it out and look at the mask again. I can practically hear the rustle of silk and see elegant dancers swirling in pairs. Will Adam be one of the Broadway guest stars? I would *so* love to go!

Will Carson stops by on the way to his locker. He's wearing his usual band logo T-shirt — Modest Mouse, whose name seems to suit his don't-look-at-me bangs and shy manner. "What's that?" he says, looking over my shoulder. I show him the poster, feeling suddenly super self-conscious. Will and I like each other, more than a little and maybe a lot, which makes things that used to be normal feel totally awkward.

Am I blushing? I hope not.

"This looks mad cool," says Will, scanning the poster. "I've heard of this Dreamcatcher band."

The date is next Friday, I notice — the day before Halloween. I also see there's a website, and make a mental note to look it up when I get home. Will gets to the bottom and lets out a low whistle. "A hundred and fifty bucks, whoa."

He's pointing at the discount price, the one that's for couples. Will darts a quick look at me, then looks away fast. Great, now we're *both* blushing.

"Are you going to lunch or the band room?" I ask quickly, tucking the poster on top of my afternoon books.

"Lunch," says Will, mumbling a quick "See you there" before scuttling off to his locker.

See you *there*? Really? I'm going there too, duh. So couldn't we walk down the staircase together, like we used to before all this liking-each-other stuff got in the way and made everything mean much too much?

This is getting ridiculous. Aren't we just friends, plus a little bit extra?

That "little bit extra" is killer.

• • •

I always eat lunch with the same three friends: Jess of course, Sara Parvati, and Amelia Williams. Overachiever Sara and sporty Amelia are each other's besties, just like me and Jess, and the four of us love to hang out as a group. But lately our table has swelled to include Will, Ethan Horowitz, who's been my friend since forever, and — this is the deal breaker — Ethan's girlfriend, Kayleigh Carell.

Kayleigh leans over the table, flipping her blond hair away from her face with one hand as she looks at the Hunger Unmasked poster sitting on top of my math book.

"Oh, the *masquerade* ball," she says, putting her other hand on Ethan's arm. "We've got tickets for that, don't we, Ethan?" Sometimes Kayleigh seems to be running her own private contest to see how many times she can use the word "we" in a sentence. Everyone gets it, okay? You're a *couple*. Big whoop.

I look down the table at Will, who's best friends with Ethan and doesn't like Kayleigh much better than I do. He's dredging a buffalo wing through blue cheese dressing.

But Kayleigh's not done yet. "My parents already bought

tickets for us," she says, smirking at me. "They're really expensive."

Just then Amelia comes back from the hot lunch line with a tray full of popcorn shrimp, wax beans, and corn.

"Where'd you get *that*?" she says, eyeing the poster as she settles down at the end of the table. "My sister's dance school is performing at this."

"The Fleet Feet Dancers?" Jess asks her, at the same time as I ask, "What stars are coming from *Angel*?"

"Fleet Feet, right. No idea what stars — if they knew, you can bet it would be on the poster," Amelia says calmly, answering both of our questions at once. She pops a shrimp into her mouth. "Ooh, hot," she says, fanning her mouth with one hand. "My mother is making me volunteer at this thing."

My ears prick up. "Really? Do they need more volunteers?"

"I can ask, but I totally doubt it," Amelia says. "Mom's drafted every kid in Fleet Feet who won't be on the stage. Plus me."

"Hey, if you want to trade places," says Jess, "I'd love to get a free pass to this. So would Diana."

Amelia shakes her head glumly. "No way I can get out of this one."

"So we'll see you there," Kayleigh says brightly, draping her arm around Ethan's neck as she beams at Amelia. "That is so *fun*!"

I'm sorry, but there's something wrong with a world where Kayleigh Carrell gets to go to a glamorous masquerade ball — possibly with *Adam Kessler* as a special guest — and Jess and I don't. I must look way disappointed, because Amelia studies my face as she finishes chewing her shrimp. Then she says, "Let me talk to my mom," in a voice that sounds more like, "we'll work something out."

CANDY APPLE BOOKS
Read them all!

Drama Queen

I've Got a Secret

Confessions of a Bitter
Secret Santa

Super Sweet 13

The Boy Next Door

The Sister Switch

Snowfall Surprise

Rumor Has It

The Sweetheart Deal

The Accidental
Cheerleader

The Babysitting Wars

Star-Crossed

Accidentally
Fabulous

Accidentally
Famous

Accidentally
Fooled

Accidentally
Friends

How to Be a Girly Girl in
Just Ten Days

Miss Popularity

Miss Popularity
Goes Camping

Making Waves

Juicy Gossip

Life, Starring Me!

Callie for President

Totally Crushed

Wish You Were Here,
Liza

See You Soon,
Samantha

Miss You, Mina

Winner Takes All

POISON APPLE BOOKS

The Dead End

This Totally Bites!

Miss Fortune

Now You See Me...

THRILLING. BONE-CHILLING.
THESE BOOKS HAVE BITE!